THE GIRL

FROM CHAPEL HILL

HER JOURNEY OF FAITH, FORGIVENESS, AND FREEDOM

12/3/22

Enjoy your journey!

vmwill

A Novel

Vanester M. Williams

ISBN 978-1-63885-478-4 (Paperback)
ISBN 978-1-63885-479-1 (Digital)

Some Scripture quotations are taken from The Holy Bible.
King James Version

Some Scripture quotations are taken from The Holy Bible,
New International Version

This novel is a work of fiction. Names, characters, places, and
incidents are either the product of the author's imagination or
are used fictitiously. Any resemblance to actual events, locals,
organizations, or persons, living or dead, is entirely coincidental and
beyond the intent of either the author or publisher.

Covenant Books, Inc.
11661 Hwy 707
Murrells Inlet, SC 29576
www.covenantbooks.com

To my husband, Rick
You are my best friend, my confidante,
my quiet and funny cheerleader.
Thank you for always being here for me.
Your patience and untiring support gently
steer me along each and every day.
I am so grateful to God for having you as my life partner!

*****

To my grandmother, Laura E. Malone (in memory)
My champion, my role model
Thank you for being such a beacon of light
You will forever live on in my heart!

ACKNOWLEDGMENTS

Foremost and above all, I acknowledge my Heavenly Father. If it wasn't for His love, support, wisdom, and guidance, the completion of this book certainly would not have been made possible. Throughout this process, I asked for and received His guidance and wisdom in so many unexpected ways!

Special appreciation for editorial reviews: Yvonne Coates, Pam Getch, Greg Mills, Alicia Nelson, and Byron Williams.

A special thanks go to the following persons for encouraging me along this journey and not giving up on me. They prayed for me, served as my sounding boards, and participated in so many other acts of kindness. They never, ever made me feel like pursuing this dream was "just a passing fancy."

Dr. Daniel and Tammie Floyd, Pastors and my Lifepoint Church Family, Fredericksburg, Virginia

Dr. Betty J. Swinney, Pastor, Outreach Christian Center, Clinton, Maryland

My daughter and son-in-law, Dana Marie and Keith Harris

My son and daughter-in-law, Jeremy and Renata Williams

My grandson and granddaughter, Dominic and Zoë Grace

My goddaughter and godson-in-law, Tarsha and Ben Wells

My godsons and goddaughter-in-law, Jonathan Davis, Matthew Gooding, Michael and Jaye Smith,

And Dr. Cecillia Fletcher

PROLOGUE

Her mama was an incredibly strong, influential, God-fearing, and loving Christian woman. The girl from Chapel Hill, now all grown up and living in a small rural town in Ohio, would later come to appreciate her mama's wonderful qualities. In a life so filled with twists and turns, she would eventually find herself drawing on the many lessons learned from her mama. Yes, one day, she would come to embrace the faith that Mama cherished. However, growing up in a small country town in northeastern Tennessee, the girl didn't think too much about how valuable these childhood lessons would be in shaping her future and equipping her for the road she was destined to travel.

Life would take her on a journey filled with so many challenges, so much so that even her very existence would be threatened. Yet through them all, one thing remains steady—the everlasting presence of God!

If you ever see her around town, just smile and say hello. Oh, and just in case you are wondering, yes, this girl, no matter how old she becomes, will always respond favorably to being called "the girl from Chapel Hill."

1

On this brisk autumn Saturday morning, the girl finds herself standing on the edge of a riverbank, reflecting on the many lessons she learned from Mama. As she gazes up to catch the sunrise slowly come into focus, glad that the fog is finally lifting, she enjoys the stillness of the moment. She is surrounded by beautiful mountains and bright foliage. Laura, the girl from Chapel Hill, inhales the crisp fresh air and, without thinking, shakes her hair to rid it of some fallen leaves that had drifted from the nearby trees. This riverbank spot is one of her favorite escape places.

Suddenly engulfed with precious childhood memories, she begins to reflect on where she is, where she has come from, and the uncertainty of where life appears to be taking her. Laura faces some turmoil in her life. She wonders what advice Mama would have given her.

"I miss you, Mama," she mumbles.

Laura would oftentimes be referred to as the girl from Chapel Hill, who could be heard repeating, "You know what Mama always said." Looking back over her life, she reflects on how Mama, who had limited resources, always tried to teach her the most important traits that define a person's character. Mama taught her that it isn't the amount of money in one's possession, nor is it the type of house one lives in that defines a person. She taught her that it isn't the style of clothing one wears, nor the type of formal education one has completed that makes the difference.

Mama would say, "Ask yourself this question, long after you are gone, what will people remember about your character? That's what defines a person. That's what makes a person unique." Mama taught her these invaluable lessons and so many more.

Last Saturday, as Laura was coming out of the grocery store, the stranger had come seemingly out of nowhere. He approached her with some shocking information about her family's history. Taken back by his abrupt appearance and the manner in which he had called out to her, she initially thought he had mistaken her for someone else. There was something ever so slightly familiar about him, but she couldn't quite place what it was. Who was this stranger? Where had he come from? How could he know so much about her and her family? Laura quickly scanned her surroundings as the stranger started to approach. With some apprehension, she paused in her tracks. She noticed that this stranger didn't introduce himself, but after calling out her full name, he immediately began to provide some facts about her that got her attention right away. He then shared the shocking news that left Laura questioning her very identity. He didn't give her a chance to ask him anything. He informed her that—for now—it was important to keep this information to herself. Then just as quickly as he had approached, he left, ending the brief one-way conversation by saying he would contact her later with further details and directions. Stunned and speechless, she watched the back of this stranger as he walked away. Her mind was immediately filled with all sorts of questions.

Wait, how will he be able to get in touch with me later? Does he have my phone number? Does he know where I work or even know where I live? Did he just tell me to keep this information to myself? Surely, he doesn't intend for me to with-hold this information from my husband?

The encounter with the stranger had left Laura feeling like she was stepping out of the pages of a really bad novel or worse, scrambling to wake up from a horrible nightmare. If the stranger's information was based on facts, Laura knew her mind would soon find its way frantically going down a rabbit hole in search of "who am I?" Puzzled and shaken, she finally made it to her car. Before driving off, she looked around again to see if she could even get a glimpse of this stranger. Just that quick, he was nowhere to be seen. She made some efforts to pull herself together and eventually headed straight for home, forgetting that she had several other errands to run.

Here it is, exactly one week since her encounter with the stranger. She is still waiting to hear from him.

Why did he tell me not to mention this to anyone? Why wouldn't I share this with my husband? Laura keeps wondering.

She pulls her cloak more closely around her to ward off the chilly wind that unexpectedly picks up where she is standing near the riverbank. Her thoughts take her back to a particular moment in time. She's thinking about a con-versation she had with Mama many, many years ago. As the two of them were watching one of those old black-and-white Westerns on television, a commercial came on the air. All of a sudden, Mama became noticeably upset and muttered something about wishing people would take responsibilities for their actions regardless of who they are or the sacrifices they may need to make. When Laura asked her what she meant, Mama looked stunned as if she hadn't intended to speak her thoughts out loud. She stared at Laura for a brief moment, shook her head, and quickly left the room. *What just happened?* Laura remembers thinking. However, Mama never provided any explanation about what she said or why she reacted as she did. And that was the end of that!

Laura hadn't thought much about that incident since she was a child. Why did these thoughts unexpectedly come to the forefront of her mind? Were there hints in that incident that could paint a clearer picture of what Laura faces now? Had Mama ever alluded to anything remotely related to this stranger's news? She's pondering over whether there were any other occasions where anyone might have said something that provided any insight regarding the shocking news delivered by this stranger.

Did Mama have a clue? "Oh, Mama, how I wish you were still here with me," moans Laura.

Mama would have known what to do, for in Laura's mind, it seemed she always knew exactly what to do. Laura's dear Mama had died several years back, and now the girl from Chapel Hill was left with more questions than answers. All the lessons Mama had taught the girl were like precious jewels.

Facing this latest turmoil, Laura now knows without a doubt that she has to hold on to these treasured lessons, these jewels, to survive, especially with so many ups and downs, twists and turns in her life.

Laura was reared by her grandmother (whom she affectionately calls Mama) from birth. For some reason, early in life, she had been led to believe Mama took her in when she was two months old. It wasn't until after Laura was married that she found out, undoubtedly by chance, that Mama had, in fact, reared her from birth. Laura's mother, Rebecca, visited her as often as she could. So although Laura calls her Becky, she acknowledges their relationship. Becky always strived to show love and support to Laura, regardless of what life threw at her. From early on, Laura had learned that sometimes, life throws you a bad curve and you have got to do the next best thing to stay in the game. Somehow, this girl from Chapel Hill knew that was exactly what happened to her mother at the time she was born. It wasn't something that was discussed around the dinner table, but Laura knew.

Laura's memory of Mama and just how much she was missed takes her back to another pivotal moment in time.

It was an early morning hospital visit, and she found herself facing perhaps one of the most painful experiences of her life. It was about fifteen years ago, and Laura was standing beside Mama's bedside in the intensive care unit of a major city hospital.

Anyway, in that hospital room as she stood there watching Mama slowly slip away, for the doctors had put her on life support, tears began to quickly flow down Laura's face. Laura's thinking back to the day before this particular hospital visit when the family had gathered for a "special meeting" to come to grips with a crucial decision, whether or not to take the doctors' advice and have the life support machines disconnected from Mama.

Laura thinks about how the family had been told that all of her bodily organs were rapidly deteriorating, that she was nonresponsive, and that it would be only a matter of days.

So there Laura stood, gazing down at Mama, barely able to see clearly due to the overflow of tears. Childhood flashbacks raced through her mind. She listened to the sounds of the beeps from the various monitors and watched Mama's chest rise and fall ever so slightly. She recalled how thankful she was for the precious little time she had been afforded to have Mama all to herself during that early morning hospital visit. Even though the doctors had informed the family that Mama was now in a coma, Laura grabbed a hold of those precious moments to spend some private time with her and let her know how much she loved and appreciated her. Laura couldn't help but reflect on all Mama meant to her. No, Mama was not a saint, but in Laura's mind, she would always be close to one. Mama was the one who instilled the morals and values that shaped her into the person she is today.

Laura recalls how Mama always taught her to obey the golden rule, to treat people like she wanted to be treated. In her mind, she hears more of her favorite sayings, "Be careful how you treat people on your way up, for you might meet those same people on your way down," "always respect your elders," "be sensitive to the needs of others," and that "a white lie was still a lie, no matter who said it."

Leaning over Mama in that hospital bed, Laura's memories continue to run rampant. She taught her that it doesn't matter how far you go, just as long as you remember from where you came. She remembers Mama teaching her that to gain respect, you have got to give respect. She even thinks about all the times Mama told her to put God first in everything and to always lean on Him.

"Oh, Mama, thank you," cries Laura as the tears continue to flow.

After the death of her grandfather when she was thirteen, she always believed it was Mama (the matriarch) who held the family together.

Laura will always be grateful that God afforded her the much-needed opportunity to truly see just how special her relationship was with Mama. For you see, as Laura continued to stand by Mama's bedside, leaning in closely while talking to her, telling her how much she appreciated her, and thanking her for all she had ever done for her, something so special, so significant, so miraculous happened in that hospital room, something that Laura will always hold dear to her heart. For not only did Mama mean so much to Laura, apparently Laura held a special place in Mama's heart as well. As Mama laid there unconscious and Laura continued to pour out her love and gratitude toward her, Mama gently squeezed her hand, gradually opened her eyes, and looked directly at this girl from Chapel Hill. There was no mistaking that physical and spiritual connection in that hospital room on that very early morning. Laura felt compelled to motion to a nurse who was standing nearby to witness that moment, a moment that only lasted for about the span of five minutes. She didn't think anyone would ever believe what had just happened. Then without saying a single word, Laura knew, she just knew with complete assurance that Mama had heard her and also understood what she was trying to tell her.

Laura also knew that Mama was at peace. For as she gradually closed her eyes again, Laura found comfort in knowing that Mama would soon be resting in the arms of her Jesus. She smiled through all the tears and affectionately remembered one thing Mama never did as she went about her business. She never wasted precious time getting there.

By the way, Laura will always be grateful that God took the decision to have Mama taken off life support out of the family's hands. Before the doctor got the opportunity to disconnect the life support machines, she went home to be with the Lord.

Even though that early morning hospital visit happened so many years earlier, it is still fresh in Laura's mind as she stands by the edge of the riverbank. Just at that exact moment, several birds land on some treetops nearby and start chirping. As they begin to fly away, Laura finds herself smiling. She remembers how she loved to bird-watch with Mama. The two of them would play a game of trying to guess what song the birds were singing. She gazes toward heaven and silently thanks Mama for the memory.

Memories of Mama temporarily fade as her mind returns to her current situation. Laura knows she is standing at a crossroad in her life, and that the clock is ticking. Looking out over that riverbank, she takes a deep breath, stoops down, picks up a couple of nearby stones, and throws them into the river, enjoying the rippling effects. She then stands up straight, wipes away the tears that had suddenly threatened to overtake her emotions, leans her head back, and exits her solitary escape place.

While birds continue to sing off in the distance, she knows she is no closer to understanding the matter that is haunting her the most. How can she successfully move on to the next chapter in her life without having resolution of the current daunting issues?

2

Shortly after arriving home from her riverbank escape spot, Laura rushes to answer the telephone, only to find it is another of those unidentified calls. After hanging up, her mind takes her back to the previous unidentified calls. Most of them were the same; there was heavy breathing on the other end of the line, and she could also hear a clicking sound. Then the caller would abruptly hang up. The first call, which started about one month before the stranger had approached her, was a little different. During that call, she had heard several people conversing on the other end of the line, then the phone went silent. After the second unidentified call, she had contacted her husband, Andrew (Drew), and told him about them. She also told him how uncomfortable they made her feel. He sounded like he was rushing off to a meeting or something. He merely suggested that perhaps they were just prank calls from teenagers. Perplexed, she couldn't understand how he could so casually dismiss her concerns.

Lately, with their hectic schedules, they rarely have time to spend with each other. She recalls their last conversation before he left for his overseas business trip. She had snapped at him about not repairing one of the kitchen drawers. He had snapped back that he would get to it when he has more time.

She remembers thinking, *This is such a petty, ridiculous argument. These "petty arguments" seem to be occurring more regularly. There's something seriously wrong with our relationship.* She knows his long-term travels as a software engineer consultant don't help, but she also admits to being partly to blame. She has a tendency to shut down when he attempts to get her to open up and communicate, particularly during this time of the year. Yes, she's worried that their marriage of twenty-four years may be in trouble.

Even still, she assumes he would have at least pretended to care more about her welfare when she expressed concern over the calls. After the phone conversation with him, she was feeling even more isolated.

Her thoughts rotate between the disturbing phone calls and her marriage. At first, the calls were annoying. Now they are becoming increasingly disturbing. Laura has a tendency to handle things on her own. So she's still trying to decide whether she's making a big deal out of the phone calls or if she should contact the police. The calls only happen when she's home alone, causing her imagination to go into overdrive.

Does anyone know I'm home alone? Is someone stalking me? With Drew away, the house is too quiet. This time, he's expected to be gone for about three weeks.

During the first couple years of their marriage, they had enjoyed spending more time traveling together. They had fun, laughing at each other's jokes.

Where is the laughter now? thinks Laura. She misses the laughter; she misses him.

Then her thoughts turn to their three sons and how much she adores them! The twenty-two-year-old twins, Matthew (Matt) and Martin (Marty), graduated from college about one year ago. They've always been extremely close, and so it wasn't a surprise when they announced their plans to share an apartment after graduation. Both of them are working and enjoying their independence. Their youngest son, Michael (Mike), is a nineteen-year-old sophomore at Smithdeal-Madison University. His school is about two hours away from home.

Laura can't help but laugh when she thinks about some of the sibling rivalry that occurred while the boys were living at home. From Boy Scouts to Little League baseball, from football to soccer, there was always somewhere to go, always something to keep them busy! It seemed their home was usually the one to host sleepovers, backyard cookouts, etc. Now as she walks from the kitchen to the family room, where she stares at their photos on the wall and back to the kitchen again, she finds herself missing those days. The house certainly wasn't quiet then. There was always laugher and never a dull moment. She misses the noise and the madness. She misses her boys.

The ringing of the phone startles her, but she decides not to answer it this time. Dealing with the aftermath of the stranger's shocking news combined with the disturbing phone calls, she is beginning to suffer from sleep deprivation and anxiety. Another forlorn day comes to an end, so she retires to their upstairs bedroom and does her normal routine. As usual, it's difficult for her to fall asleep, so she takes a couple of sleeping pills.

Sundays without Drew are particularly lonely. After a restless night, she goes downstairs to fix herself a light breakfast. Childhood flashbacks of Sunday mornings always make her hungry. For as long as she can remember, on Sunday mornings, she can't help but think about Mama's huge country breakfasts. There was always someone from the neighborhood or other family members stopping by to enjoy a feast of bacon, sausage, grits, eggs, fried apples, old-fashioned home fries, and Mama's famous homemade sweet potato biscuits. After breakfast, they would walk across the road to church. Other than on those rare occasions when Laura might have had an earache or some other minor ailment, she can't recall not going to church on Sundays. When she thinks about how she tried to carry a tune when singing in the church choir, she laughs out loud.

Warm memories take her back to the summer vacation Bible school when she became a Christian and got baptized, along with several of her friends, in an outdoor pool. She was about twelve years old at the time.

Frowning now, she wonders why she stopped going to church regularly when she left home for college.

I miss getting together with people at church, she's thinking.

She hasn't taken the time to connect with other Christians on a more regular basis. More importantly, she certainly hasn't made many attempts to develop a closer relationship with God through prayer and Bible studies. Now with everything that is going on, she feels overwhelmed. She finds herself wanting to pray, to reach out to Him, but doesn't believe she's worthy of His attention.

She pauses for a brief moment and cries out, "I sure wish I knew how to talk with You now, God, for I really could use Your help!"

Little did Laura know that she was actually praying, using these simple words. However, preoccupied with her current circumstances, she doesn't take the time to hear that God is, indeed, talking back to her, telling her to be still and to trust Him.

During moments such as this one, Laura gives in to the overwhelming feelings of guilt as she continually wrestles with several issues, including not forgiving herself or others for past actions. She rationalizes that since she has not totally surrendered everything to God, He couldn't possibly have time for her. She also has misgivings about trusting others and dealing with change. She often beats up on herself, her self-esteem is at an all-time low, and she second-guesses her own self-worth and purpose in life. All of this, combined with this recent shocking news from the stranger, leaves Laura feeling as if she is on an emotional roller coaster that is about to run offtrack.

Another Sunday comes to an end, and she retires for the evening. Even though she takes a couple of sleeping pills, Laura tosses and turns throughout the night. Then there is that dream, that recurring vivid dream that she's been periodically having for years. In her dream, she hears the same weak urgent voice of a little girl crying out. Laura is frantically drifting around, sort of floating in the direction of that voice, but the voice keeps getting more distant and fainter. Then abruptly, there is silence, and everything goes black as if a light switch has been turned off. Whenever she has this dream, Laura wakes up, softly crying, perspiring, and anxious. She has never told anyone, including Drew, about this dream. This is her secret, a secret burden that weighs on her heavily, even after all these years.

The next morning, as she's driving to her job at Chestnut-Patterson University, she can't help but think that something's missing in her life. She has been employed at the university for over five years as an adjunct English professor. Until recently, she believed this was her lot in life. However, she's now having second thoughts and can't quite put her finger on the problem. She's been despondent over her job for several months, so it's not the news from the stranger.

Perhaps I need to look at a different career path. I'm just not sure. But with the latest news, I'm sure this isn't the appropriate time to make such a decision, she thinks.

As soon as she gets to her classroom, Laura develops an unrelenting migraine headache. She has a difficult time concentrating on anything, much less work. During autumn season, her headaches usually get worse. Earlier last week, she had spoken with her boss about the need to possibly take a leave of absence. So when the day comes to an end, it is no surprise when she gives notice that she has a personal emergency and needs to take a three-month hiatus. Unfortunately, now feeling quite overwhelmed, Laura knows she needs some quality time, especially away from prying eyes, to deal with all this. As an extremely private person, this girl from Chapel Hill has a tendency to internalize everything and, in addition to her current situation, is still reeling from previous emotional struggles, some due to poor judgment.

Driving home from work, Laura's thoughts continue to run wild.

What would provoke a stranger to approach me with this news, particularly at this time after all these years? Is there any connection between the relentless disturbing phone calls and his news? Survival mode is kicking in; Laura's trying hard not to go overboard and drown in her own troublesome thoughts.

At home, she is still unable to focus, especially with the ongoing disturbing phone calls and the nagging thoughts about everything that appears to be unfolding at this time. She feels like the house is closing in on her (or maybe it is life itself), so she considers a brief getaway.

I need to get away from this house. A change of venue should be good, she thinks.

She calls Drew and unable to get him on the phone, she decides to leave him a message.

Do I tell him about the stranger? Do I let him know I'm feeling overwhelmed and need to take some time off from work? Do I tell him about my long-kept secret? In the end, she simply leaves him a message that says she needs to take about three months off from work due to stress and will share more when he calls her back.

She contemplates whether to drive to the Regal Bay Resort (an oceanfront area) about three hours away. One of her colleagues had recommended this resort as the perfect getaway spot—one intended for solitude, relaxation, and reflection. The girl from Chapel Hill could never decide, which she preferred while vacationing, being near the ocean or surrounded by mountains. She loves the tranquility of both scenes, but for some unknown reason, this time, she feels drawn to the ocean. After taking care of some house-keeping chores, she packs a suitcase containing enough clothing for one week and decides to drive to the resort the next morning. After talking with her colleague, she had done her own research and discovered that this place was extremely popular, especially around this time of the year. So she was enormously pleased to be able to get a room at the last minute.

Later that night, she calls Drew again—no answer. So she leaves him a message that she's leaving for the Regal Bay Resort Hotel in the morning and plans to stay there for about one week.

She's thinking to herself, *Even though we didn't part on the best of terms, I really can't understand why I haven't heard back from him.* However, with so much on her mind, she chooses not to dwell on marital issues at this time.

After checking in with each of her boys and learning that all is well with them, she decides to call it an early night. She doesn't look forward to another restless sleep.

The next morning, Laura arrives at the hotel—some-what exhausted—and is elated to hear she can check in earlier than twelve noon. At the check-in counter, she has an eerie feeling that someone is watching her. She looks around and sees several people hovering nearby, appearing to be engaged in deep conversations. However, since her nerves are already on edge, she attributes this feeling to her mind working overtime and shrugs it off, taking the elevator to her second-floor room.

After settling into her hotel room, unable to take a much-needed nap, Laura ventures out to grab a bite at a small coffee shop on the boardwalk. Rather than return to her hotel room, she opts to eat at the coffee shop since it has a really great view of the ocean. She had originally thought about walking the beach—just to clear her head, but she notices dark clouds are developing, and the weather's getting cooler.

Oh my, I never thought about checking the weather for this week before I picked this resort, thinks Laura.

So instead of walking the beach, she takes a corner table that is sort of hidden toward the back of the coffee shop and plans to do some reading before returning to her room.

Glancing briefly through a local newspaper while sipping tea and eating a blueberry muffin, her eyes are suddenly drawn to an interesting article about a well-known motivational speaker, who is also a clinical psychologist. This speaker (Silvia Anderson, PhD) is in town for one week and is scheduled to conduct a two-hour seminar at a Christian conference being held at the Westchester Palace, another nearby ocean-view hotel. The title of Dr. Anderson's seminar, *The Battles Within: Enough is Enough*, captures her attention, and surprisingly, Laura is debating on whether she should attend. She is not accustomed to making hasty decisions, particularly when she's overly stressed. However, for some reason, she decides to register for this seminar that is scheduled for the next morning. While this seminar may or may not help her with all of the cobwebs of questions buzzing through her head, it might be a refreshing distraction from all life's drama.

Sounds crazy, right? thinks Laura, shaking her head.

Little did she know that this was exactly what she needed, a diversion for such a time as this.

Leaving the coffee shop, Laura returns to the hotel lobby and hesitates, again sensing she is being either followed or watched.

There doesn't appear to be a lot of people circulating in the lobby, so she asks herself, "Am I really that paranoid?"

Attempting to shrug off the feeling, she tightens the grip on her purse and heads to her room.

Back in her room, she orders a light dinner from the hotel restaurant. She is browsing through a couple of the hotel tourist attraction magazines when she believes she hears a scraping noise at her door. However, when she looks through the peephole, she sees no one. Opening the door and looking down the hallway, she sees the back of a person briskly walking away. She decided not to call after the person, guessing whoever it was had gotten her room mixed up for someone else's.

Laura tries to relax amidst her anxiety. Although exhausted, she's still not able to easily fall to sleep. So she decides to drink some tea and channel surf. Not such a great idea, for as she flips through the channels, her eyes land on an old Western show that causes her to pause, thinking about Mama and that long-ago incident.

"Not tonight," moans Laura as she quickly turns off the television.

She finishes her tea and double-checks to make sure the door is securely locked. Finally, she pops a couple of sleeping pills and gets into bed, only to dream about Western shows, Mama, the stranger, hearing a little girl crying out "Mommy," the phone calls, and her husband, all converging as one in her dreams. Restful sleep was not to befriend her tonight.

3

After getting dressed, she walks the short distance to the hotel where the conference is being held at 9:00 a.m. She arrives a little earlier than anticipated, grabs a cup of coffee, and immediately begins to have second thoughts about attending.

After all, I don't know why I am here. What has provoked me to attend this conference and especially sign up for this particular seminar? I've attended several types of these conferences before. How will this one be any different? What in the world was I thinking?

However, for some unknown reason, she feels compelled to stick out this one. Even still, after locating the conference room where the seminar is being held, she quickly grabs a seat near the back of the room just in case she decides to make a quick escape. Looking around, she is not surprised to see a large number of seminar attendees—both men and women. After all, the speaker was well-known and had written several best-seller inspirational books. Reluctant to admit, even to herself, Laura is happy that there are no familiar faces among the attendees. Being an introvert, she has no interest in chatting with acquaintances about what led her to come here, especially when she doesn't have a clue. Nor does she desire to indulge in any annoying chitchats merely intended to take up time while waiting for the seminar to start.

As the seminar gets underway, Laura's thoughts trail off but are quickly brought back to the present when Dr. Anderson says something that catches her attention.

"Don't allow your past to define who you are…and to move forward. It is important to conquer your worst enemy." Dr. Anderson appears to be setting the atmosphere for some type of self-evaluation exercise. Laura sits up straight and leans in even more as she listens to what the speaker is saying.

"The great apostle Paul knew something about this subject when he wrote in the Bible, *I find then a law, that, when I would do good, evil is present with me* [Romans 7:21 KJV]. How often are you plagued with the constant battle that rages within you, the battle of the wills? Should I or should I not? Rather than wrestle with these demons, you must learn to live in the posture of 'Lord, not my will, but thou will be done.' Know this—when you yield to the wonderful gift of His precious Holy Spirit, you will be able to boldly make a wholehearted, sincere determination that regardless of the circumstances, you will not be subjected to the battles within! These battles will succumb to the will of the Master!"

Dr. Anderson ends her introduction by saying, "It is my goal that the materials covered during this seminar will awaken something within you that will propel you to rise up against any challenge you encounter. It is my goal that this seminar will help you stand up in your God-given image and with complete boldness say to the battles that lie within you, 'Enough is enough!'"

Well, She unintentionally chuckles to herself. "I am not quite sure what all of this means, but I do feel like I am in a battle right now." She's thinking, *Battle or not, again, why am I here? How is listening to all of this fixing my problems? What has all of this got to do with anything?* She is about to jump ship—make a fast exit when the next words from the speaker almost literally hold her spellbound to her seat.

"There has got to come a time in your life when you firmly plant yourself on solid ground and with bold determination say, 'Enough is enough. I will not be ruled by how I feel, I will not be ruled by what I see, I will not be ruled by what others say or don't say, and I will not be moved by what others do or don't do.' There has got to come a time in your life when you set yourself and say, 'It doesn't matter how long I am standing, it doesn't matter whether I am standing alone, I will not be moved! I will not be moved by anything that goes contrary to the Word of God. I simply will not be moved! Enough is enough!' There has got to come a time in your life when you set yourself and say, 'God has given me everything I need to be victorious in this situation, for God has already defeated the enemy! Enough is enough!' There has got to come a time in your life when you say to yourself, 'I will not just be a hearer of the Word, I will be an active participant.' There has got to come a time in your life when you say to yourself, 'I will allow the Word to become alive in me, and I will become a doer of the Word.' Then you will believe without a shadow of a doubt that no weapon formed against you will prosper.

"When your heart aligns with His Spirit, there is no limit to the blessings that lay in store for you. Circumstances won't move you. Your mind will be conditioned to trust in Him, for there will be no question that all your needs will be met in God's timetable. That's right. The Bible lets us know that God's timing is not our timing. Are you willing to wait on God? Or will you continue to live your life being ruled by the battles within?

"I'd like you to pause for about five minutes to digest what all of this may mean."

"Ruled by the battles within," Laura says to herself. While she didn't quite understand the meaning of such catchy jargon used by the speaker, she knows her response to the question, "Are you willing to wait on God?" was probably a resounding no. Patience had never been one of her better qualities. Admittedly, Laura knows she has a lot to learn about faith, especially trusting in a God she couldn't see. Also, since she was never one who believed in attending church regularly, she has more questions than answers when it comes to the Bible. While it is true that she had previously attended several Christian conferences, it was mainly because some friend or acquaintance had arm-wrestled her into doing so. Deep down, she reminded herself that she genuinely wanted to learn how to communicate with God, but more often than not, she hadn't made a concerted effort to do so because she allowed life to get in the way.

Thinking back to when she was growing up, Laura recalls how she would often take a glimpse inside the covers of the Bible that Mama continuously kept by her bedside. A lot of what she had read appeared foreign to her.

4

The material covered so far in the seminar gives Laura quite a bit to consider. Taking advantage of Dr. Anderson's five-minute break, Laura decides to put the pin to paper regarding some of her thoughts.

She notes, "Dr. Anderson is a great teacher who knows how to take command of her audience without coming across as pushy or aggressive. She seems to genuinely care about each one of us. Whatever seems to be motivating her is a gift to be envied. Yes, there's something about her that gently presses upon me a desire to want to learn more, to want to be better. There's something about her presentation that gives me hope for a brighter future regardless of my past, regardless of present circumstances."

After the brief pause, Dr. Anderson takes a sip of her water, flips through her notes, and smiles as she gazes out at her audience. She appears to be looking directly at Laura as she poses a series of questions.

"Are you finally ready to face your worst enemy? Are you sure? Are you ready to take this first step regardless of what you may find? Okay then, get ready, get set. Try this—close your eyes for a moment and imagine you are looking into a mirror at this very moment. Take a step closer, don't be shy. Now take your time and look at who's facing you. Look at the image in the mirror. Are you finally ready to be true to yourself? Believe it or not, what you see is not an illusion. Your worst enemy is staring right back at you. Are you surprised? When all is said and done, you, my friend, are the one who started the whole thing. You are the one who opened the door to the enemy. Yes, you are the one who gave him an open invitation. You are the one who allowed him to dine at your table. You are the one who made him feel so comfortable that he has no desire to leave. You are the one who even invited him to bring along his guests! An open invitation from you, your worst enemy! And you thought it was somebody else. Can you boldly face your worst enemy? Go ahead, take a long, hard look— eyeball to eyeball—and stare yourself down. Can you do it?

"To borrow a quote from someone very special to me, 'Are you willing to speak things to that enemy in the mirror that you simply will not allow any other person to say to you?' What's the matter? Are you afraid of what your reaction may reveal? Are you afraid of what you may uncover? This sounds crazy, doesn't it? But wait a minute! Stay with me here and let's examine where you are at this exact moment. Let's take a mental survey."

Surprisingly, Laura finds herself preparing to take this interesting mental survey. She simply can't believe what is happening! Sitting in the seminar, it appears an internal switch has flipped. This girl from Chapel Hill had never heard anyone break down these Scriptures in such a way that she can truly understand and apply them to her life.

"What have I been missing?" she asks herself. Laura admits she was beginning to enjoy Dr. Anderson's plain and simple teaching mannerism and realizes she is eagerly looking forward to hearing more. Without knowing it, this seminar was predestined to change her life and to give her the emotional and spiritual strength needed for what she was about to face in the not-too-distant future.

Dr. Anderson continues by challenging the attendees to be honest with themselves in taking this survey. She also asks them to commit to starting a journal regarding their daily actions pertaining to the questions presented.

"Are you renewing your mind daily? Well, this may sound unnecessary, but don't let your thoughts wander here. Stay focused. It may be in the middle of the day and you are at work. Not only are you facing a mountain of tasks at hand, but you are surrounded by a lot of gossiping people who are exhibiting all sorts of negative energy. Deep down, you wished you were somewhere else. You simply are tired of being tired. It seems yesterday's tasks lingered over into today. Today's problems aren't being resolved and have the potential to carry over into tomorrow. Instead of embracing tomorrow, you are dreading it. You want out of this rat race, but the bills keep coming. The mountain of debt doesn't seem to be diminishing.

"Are you able to wrap your mind around the fact that perhaps God placed you exactly where He wants you to be at this precise moment, for such a time as this? Have you considered this—it is time to grow up spiritually, it is time to rise to the challenge, it is time for a shake-up, and it is time for a mental makeover. It is time to finally present yourself in a manner pleasing to God so that He gets the Glory out of it all.

"Remember, the Bible states, '*For I know the plans I have for you,*' *declares the* LORD, '*plans to prosper you and not to harm you, plans to give you hope and a future*' [Jeremiah 29:11 NIV]. He knows the course He's chartered for you. Are you ready to change focus and be an available, willing vessel He wants to use? Yes, even at the workplace. It is all up to you. Instead of getting all worked up because no one's listening to your point of view, instead of complaining because it doesn't appear anything is going your way, instead of tossing in the towel because your team didn't deliver that project on time and under budget, change your mindset. Instead of joining in on all the office gossip, instead of mumbling, grumbling, and complaining about everything that is not going right, change your focus.

"Are you ready to exercise your mind? Do you truly want to redirect that negative energy filled with such evil, selfish, and derogative thoughts? Are you ready to listen to someone else's point of view about the entire matter? Then who better to listen to than the One who blessed you with that job? Then who better to listen to than the One who allowed you to get up each morning and be at that job? Then who better to listen to you than the One who created you and continues to sustain you second by second? When all is said and done, who are you really working for after all? *Come on now, let this mind be in you that was also in Christ Jesus* [Philippians 2:5].

"This calls for a shifting of your very mental makeup. This is the time when you need to reel in your thoughts, forget about yourself, and all that is not happening to your satisfaction. This is the time when you need to focus on what the apostle Paul challenges in the Bible, *Finally, brethren, whatsoever things are true, whatsoever things are honest, whatsoever things are just, whatsoever things are pure, whatsoever things are lovely, whatsoever things are of good report, if there be any virtue, and if there be any praise, think on these things* [Philippians 4:8 KJV].

"Are you willing to do whatever it takes to renew your mind daily? Just as you would train your body to run in an Olympic race, you must train and condition your mind to live a life free of worries. You must condition your mind to live a life full of joy and peace. If you continually allow your environment to conform you rather than allow your environment to conform to a positive mindset, you will remain carnally minded. All your thoughts will be on what you believe the world owes you. Simply put, all your thoughts will be on "you, yourself, and yours." Are you a carnally minded person? Remember now, you are facing your worst enemy.

Are you a double-minded person, unstable in all your ways, carried to and fro with everything that comes your way only to find out later that you were fooled by a wolf in sheep's clothing? In a world so filled with negative happenings, in a world so filled with unhappiness and a hopeless generation, in a world so filled with darkness, don't you believe it is time to change your focus? It is time that your mind be renewed so you can be that light that draws men to Christ. The Bible states, *And be not conformed to this world: but be ye transformed by the renewing of your mind, that ye*

THE GIRL FROM CHAPEL HILL

may prove what is that good, and acceptable, and perfect, will of God [Romans 12:2 KJV]. If you are not renewing your mind daily, you are your worst enemy!"

So far, the information presented during the seminar has been enlightening, and Laura really wants to believe that it is not too late for her to make a change.

Am I my worst enemy? Is this why I beat up on myself so often? Am I ready to do whatever it takes to renew my mind? thinks Laura. She chuckles to herself. "With everything that's going on in my life right now, I am amazed that I still have a mind to be renewed. I find myself now questioning my husband's love—there, I said it! I find myself wondering if my career is going in the right direction. I feel exhausted most of the time. I depend on pills to help me sleep, and even then, I twist and turn most nights—often thinking about the frightened little girl in my dreams. Above everything else, with the latest news from the stranger, I am beginning to question my very identity. Who am I? Has my entire life been a lie? Lord, help me," moans Laura.

While Laura's thoughts occasionally shift to the stranger's news or the disturbing phone calls or to her dreams (which she now calls nightmares), she finds herself clearly drawing strength from hearing the various Scriptures and the possibility of actually being able to apply them in her troublesome life. So she redirects her attention to what the speaker is now saying.

"You have faced your worst enemy, and you realize that you can't tackle the battle of the wills on your own. It is a stronghold that no human intervention can master. For with years of misuse, the fuel for sustaining this enemy has been contaminated with too many 'ITs.' What's an 'IT?' Check this out—an 'IT' is an intangible tank of nasty, evil leeching spirits that feed off each other. They aren't happy traveling solo. They aren't content being all by themselves. So they attract and retain the worst of the worst. Combined, they come to kill, steal, and destroy. But there is good news. In the Bible, Jesus said, *I came that you might have life and that you might have it more abundantly* [John 10:10 KJV]. That's our prescription for happiness straight from the master physician! Aren't you sick and fed up with these leeches hanging on to your every move, invading your every thought? Aren't you ready to kick them to the curb for once and for all and replace them with the fruit of His spirit? If you are, then let's move on and call them out! Look at it this way. In the medical profession, before a physician can diagnose an ailment, he needs to determine the cause. There can be no diagnosis without further examination. If the cause is unknown, treatment becomes a medicinal challenge.

"Okay, let's take a fifteen-minute break, and when we return, we will examine the symptoms and identify the 'IT' in your life."

5

During break time, some attendees begin conjugating and sharing some of the tidbits they had picked up from the morning's session. As a bystander, Laura remains in her seat but listens intently to what others nearby are sharing. She overhears one attendee sharing how he was particularly impressed with Dr. Anderson's definition of an intangible tank—nasty, evil leeching spirits that feed off each other. Laura does not want to join in on the conversation but admits to herself that she is interested in learning more about that as well.

Of particular interest, Laura learns that one of the attendees is a clinical psychologist who is traveling with Dr. Anderson. As it just so happens, she is staying at the same hotel where Laura is registered. Laura tucks this information away as she continues to listen in on their chattering. From the sounds of it, she takes some comfort in knowing that she's not the only one who is wrestling with the battle of the wills, internal struggles.

As an English professor, Laura can't help comparing her own teaching style to that of Dr. Anderson's.

"I could learn a lot from this speaker," she says to herself. She makes a note of the following, "I like how she is teaching. It does not make me feel gloom or doomed. Rather it is stirring something within me, causing a shift in my perspective on life. Dr. Anderson has a unique way of capturing and maintaining her audience's attention." *Wow, I am beginning to believe that it is no accident I was compelled to come to this resort during this particular week, especially with all the turmoil in my life.*

Based on this conviction, Laura smiles as she has a feeling that there is much more of this good stuff coming from Dr. Anderson. Or is it coming from another source?

Is she finally opening herself up to lean on something much bigger than herself? Something within Laura is definitely coming alive.

Dr. Anderson resumes the seminar by reminding everyone that it is time to identify their "IT" (**i**ntangible **t**ank) of nasty, evil leeching spirits that feed off each other. She then proceeds to rattle off an incomplete IT list (e.g., unforgiveness, negative confessions, bitterness, distrust, self-righteousness, and the list goes on and on).

Dr. Anderson is saying, "Time won't allow us to thoroughly discuss each of these today, but I've chosen a few for self-examination.

"Let's begin with unforgiveness. Yes, I believe this one should be at the top of our list as it alone holds the key to so many problems. Have you forgiven yourself or others for past actions? Do you believe you've done something so awful that God simply cannot forgive you?"

Without any forewarning, Laura finds herself beginning to tremble.

"Don't you dare lose it," she says to herself. She knows the topic of unforgiveness is hitting too close to home. Not only does she struggle with forgiving herself for past actions, but she also harbors resentment toward others who have wronged her. Feeling self-conscious, she looks around the room to see if anyone is staring at her, sensing her discomfort. It appears everyone is intently focused on what the speaker is about to say. So gradually, Laura's attention is redirected upfront.

"You maybe going through life at this precise moment, feeling as though you are all alone, miserable, and just downright unlovable. You have read all the 'right' books, heard some of the most uplifting songs, and perhaps listened to all sorts of inspirational-intended messages. You have even prayed and prayed and prayed. But have you ever stopped to wonder, even for a brief second, that maybe the feelings are brought on by unforgiveness, buried way deep within you? Let's call this 'hidden unforgiveness.'

"Perhaps you are going through life with some unresolved conflict within yourself. This can be your biggest downfall. Once you have asked God to forgive you, it's time to forgive yourself. You have got to resolve any remaining conflict within yourself. Stop beating up on yourself for something you did or didn't do ten, twenty, or even fifty years ago! Are you continually allowing the ghosts of your past to hover over your present and prevent you from moving on into the awesome future ordained by God?

"Are you saying that God won't forgive you? Are you saying that His Word is not true? Did you ask for forgiveness? Doesn't His Word say He would forgive you and remember your sins no more? Remember, God is not the author of confusion. The Bible instructs you to confess your sins before God, and through Jesus Christ, He will forgive you. So what are you waiting for? And if you have made this confession from your heart, then you're forgiven. Don't let the enemy steal your joy. It is Satan, not God, who keeps bringing those things of the past to the forefront of your mind. Don't give place to the enemy. God forgives, heals, and forgets. Forget those things that are behind you, the past is the past. The apostle Paul says, *Brethren, I count not myself to have apprehended: but this one thing I do, forgetting those things which are behind, and reaching forth unto those things which are before. I press toward the mark for the prize of the high calling of God in Christ Jesus* [Philippians 3:13–14 KJV].

"And listen very closely—you need to love yourself. Yes, embrace the love of God by loving yourself! Remember, how Jesus responded to a Pharisee lawyer when He was asked about the great commandment. *Jesus said unto him, Thou shalt love the Lord thy God with all thy heart, and with all thy soul, and with all thy mind. This is the first and great commandment. And the second is like unto it, Thou shalt love thy neighbour as thyself. On these two commandments hang all the law and the prophets* [Matthew 22:36–40 KJV]. So if Scriptures model the love for our neighbor as the love [we have] for ourselves, what does that tell us?"

By this time, Laura is barely able to keep it together. She starts to quietly weep and tries hard to control her sniffles. Her emotions are raw, filled with awe at how well this speaker appears to really know her. She now acknowledges that she has been struggling with truly loving herself. Based on the Scriptures just quoted by Dr. Anderson, she desires the strength to love herself so she can begin the process of loving others in a way that's pleasing to God.

"Is my life an open book?" Laura asks. "Why does it hurt so much? Is there anything I can control?" cries Laura as she continues to become unrattled.

Then a welcoming intervention occurs. Tina, the psychologist who just so happens to be staying at the same hotel as Laura, quietly comes over, sits down next to her, and gently squeezes her hand, giving her a reassuring look that implies, "I know how you must be feeling, and I am here to let you know that it is going to be okay, for you are not alone." Tina then whispers to her that she's available to meet with her afterward if she needs a listening ear. Laura sniffles, casts an appreciative look at her, takes a deep breath, and to the best of her ability, attempts to get her emotions in check. Meanwhile, Tina remains seated next to Laura, periodically giving her a reassuring, friendly look. Laura senses that she is genuine and someone who she can trust with her feelings. Since trusting others does not come easy for Laura, she takes comfort in this newfound revelation and relaxes a bit more as she turns her attention back to what Dr. Anderson is saying.

"Sure, there's a constant battle going on, even within us, the battle between good and evil. The Bible states, *For we wrestle not against flesh and blood, but against principalities, against powers, against the rulers of the darkness of this world, against spiritual hosts of wickedness in heavenly places* [Ephesians 6:12 KJV]. The Bible also says, *In the flesh, dwelleth no good thing, for even when we want to do right, evil is always present.*

"I am talking about resolving conflicts within yourself so that you can move on. The apostle Paul, who wrote over two thirds of the New Testament, instructs, *So I say, walk by the Spirit, and you will not gratify the desires of the flesh. For the flesh desires what is contrary to the Spirit, and the Spirit what is contrary to the flesh. They are in conflict with each other, so that you are not to do whatever you want. But if you are led by the Spirit, you are not under the law* [Galatians 5:16–18 NIV]."

"*So many Scriptures, so much to learn,*" Laura says to herself. She makes a mental note to dust off her Bible when she gets home as she has a strong desire to delve into some of these Scriptures.

Turning her attention upfront, she hears Dr. Anderson saying, "Now if you have accepted God's wonderful gift of salvation by accepting His Son Jesus as your Savior, then you have experienced the wonder of God's forgiveness. Therefore, you will forgive others as God has forgiven you through Christ. When you get a chance, please spend some time reading the entire passage in Matthew 18:21–35. What a wonderful example of forgiveness. Forgiving others might require an agonizing emotional struggle. It just might require fervent prayer on your part. But with the empowerment of the Holy Spirit, you can forgive.

"Here's something else to consider. Sometimes you may be unwilling 'because of pride' to realize that you may be the 'offender' and not the 'offended.' Pride is a dangerous thing. It is despised of God and will definitely keep you in bondage. Pride will keep you from enjoying all the benefits that He has in store for you. How many times have you thought back over a personal conflict where the relationship was destroyed and realized that perhaps because of your own stubbornness, your inability—or should I say your unwillingness—there are regrets? You may have regrets that you didn't do or say something differently. You may have regrets that you didn't just be still, let go and let God!

"Sometimes you take refuge behind a pretense of 'righteous indignation.' The Bible tells us that there are none righteous, no not one! Righteous indignation will say, 'Oh no, she didn't say that about me! Surely, she must be crazy! Oh my, she really needs much prayer now!' Be careful that you don't lie on the Lord. Righteous indignation will cause you to say 'the Lord told me to tell you such and such.' Be very clear here. Remember, everything you hear is not of God. Try the spirit by the spirit [His Word] and see if it is of God. Again, God is not the author of confusion. But guess who is! Remember, the spirit of God will never lead you where the Word of God cannot sustain you! If you are not sure, pray first, seek God, rest before Him, and don't you dare budge, not for one moment, until you are clear about what He wants you to do.

"Sometimes, just sometimes, we deliberately ignore a tense situation rather than praying about it and acting to resolve. Don't let conflict simmer. It is not healthy, it causes stress, which can lead to physical problems, and it will destroy you. You have got to allow the Holy Spirit to guide you. The Bible states, *Trust in the LORD with all thine heart; and lean not unto thine own understanding. In all thy ways acknowledge him, and he shall direct thy paths* [Proverbs 3:5–6, KJV]. It doesn't matter whether you're right or wrong. Allow Him to direct your path! Remember, a house divided cannot stand.

"Sometimes we believe that we are morally superior because we have found something to condemn in others. The Bible states, *Do not judge, or you too will be judged. For in the same way you judge others, you will be judged, and with the measure you use, it will be measured to you. Why do you look at the speck of sawdust in your brother's eye and pay no attention to the plank in your own eye? How can you say to your brother, 'Let me take the speck out of your eye,' when all the time there is a plank in your own eye? You hypocrite, first take the plank out of your own eye, and then you will see clearly to remove the speck from your brother's eye* [Matthew 7:1–5 KJV].

"We need to be so careful, even about our thoughts, thinking we have arrived. And oftentimes we are unable to resolve conflicts with others because we totally ignore God's Word, which specifically commands us to forgive others. *Forbearing one another, and forgiving one another, if any man has a quarrel against any, even as Christ forgave you, so also do ye* [Colossians 3:13 KJV]. Yes, I am talking about resolving conflict, even when someone has wronged you. In the Bible, Paul urges us *to live a life worthy of the calling you have received. Be completely humble and gentle, be patient, bearing with one another in love. Make every effort to keep the unity of the Spirit through the bond of peace* [Ephesians 4:1–3 NIV].

"Forgiveness is very vital if we are to be victorious! Is there someone you need to forgive today? Do you find yourself drudging up the past and refusing to forgive someone who has done you harm? Again, are you continually allowing the ghosts of your past to hover over your present and prevent you from moving on into the future that God has ordained? Why can't you believe once and for all that your past does not define the type of person you are today?

"If you are in Christ, according to the Word of God, you are a new creature. Old things are passed away. Behold all things are become new. Forgiveness—either for others or self—is not an option. According to the Bible, Jesus states, *If ye forgive not men their trespasses, neither will your Father forgive your trespasses* [Matthew 6:15 KJV]. Once you decide once and for all that you are through with being a victim of your own inability to let go of wrongs, you will be cleansed and set free to move forward. With Christ, it is not hard. But maybe you don't believe it is as simple as that?

"Remember, it is only when you experience God's grace and forgiveness in a deeply personal manner that you can be reconciled to Him. And it is only when this happens, that you will be able to extend forgiveness to others."

Dr. Anderson stares out at her audience, looks down at her watch, pauses, and instructs everyone to take a fifteen-minute break before the last IT is discussed.

6

During break time, Laura turns to Tina, who is still seated beside her and, with tears in her eyes, expresses gratitude for being there when she really needed someone to lean on. She then timidly asks her if she will have time to chat with her later today but quickly adds that she definitely understands if she's too busy. Being completely transparent, her new friend officially introduces herself as Tina Fitzgerald, a clinical psychologist, but indicates she's willing to meet with her as a confidante and not on a professional basis unless Laura wishes otherwise. After learning that they both are staying at the same hotel, Tina tentatively proposes that they meet over dinner. She informs Laura that since she's attending the conference to provide assistance to Dr. Anderson, she will need to circle back with her once she's confirmed her availability. When Laura hesitates, she provides clarification that their meeting, whenever it is, will be only between the two of them. After the break, Dr. Anderson convenes the last session by summarizing the materials covered so far. Then she shares that the last topic for today may be difficult for some but hopefully beneficial for most. This really gets everyone's full attention, so she continues.

"Do you constantly confess negativism? Are the words you say lining up with that childhood lie, 'Sticks and stones may break my bones, but words can never hurt me?' Or are they lining up with the Bible? *For by thy words thou shalt be justified and by thy words, thou shalt be condemned* [Matthew 12:37 KJV]. These words even ring true when someone is arrested. Why is it so important that the arresting officer has to state, 'You have the right to remain silent, and any words you say can and may be used against you'? Your tongue can literally condemn you in a court of law. Speaking negative words causes something to happen in the spiritual atmosphere. It inhibits the positive work of angels that have been assigned to you. How powerful are the words you speak? The Bible states, *Death and life are in the power of the tongue, and they that love it shall eat the fruit thereof* [Proverbs 18:21 KJV].

"Why not practice the silent test. There are going to be plenty of opportunities for you to practice this exercise. This practice is an exercise where you say absolutely nothing until you have received positively, no wavering, no questioning an absolute assurance of the go-ahead by the Holy Spirit. When you heed to this practice, you won't need to worry afterward about whether you should or shouldn't have said such and such. Now get this—until you have allowed the Holy Spirit to condition your mind to think only on positive things, your tongue will be unruly. Why? Because the tongue is an unruly weapon that must be tamed.

"If you are ready to unconditionally position yourself where you are no longer your worst enemy, you can begin by following the biblical example and ask the Lord to teach you to hold your tongue [Job 6:24]. You must have a teachable spirit for this to be effective. First and foremost, you have got to learn to ask God to help you overcome negative speaking. Oftentimes, we are so focused on asking God for material possessions that we don't stop to take hold of the full meaning of what it means to seek Him first. The Bible states, *But seek ye first the kingdom of God and His righteousness, and all these things shall be added unto you* [Matthew 6:33 KJV]. How often are you so focused on the *all these things shall be added* that you don't zone in on exactly what this Scripture is telling you? Well, stay with me for a moment. Remember, you are still taking a survey!

"Do you believe that asking God to teach you His ways is an example of seeking His righteousness? If so, then will you believe that asking Him to teach you to hold your tongue is one way of seeking His righteousness? Oh sure, there will come along that person who will be used to test you by saying something to get a rise out of you. How else are you going to learn to grow in His grace if you are not tested? Sure, there will come along a situation that will make you want to use all sorts of foul language or exhibit terrible behavior. But again, how else are you going to learn to grow in spiritual development?

"To purge yourself of anything that is not of God, you need to be tested. Hence, trials and tribulations will come along. Their purpose—to make you strong. Don't want to take my word for it? Just check out what the Bible has to say about this situation, *My brethren, count it all joy when ye fall into diverse temptations. Knowing this, that the trying of your faith worketh patience* [James 1:2–3 KJV].

"When someone says something unpleasant to you, are you tempted to respond in a way that you know will not be pleasing to God? Or do you count it all joy? Do their words stir up a desire in you to lash out with the same kind of venom? Or do you count it all joy? Does this try your faith in the ability of God to sustain you, to propel you, to grow you up? Do you often offend others with your own distasteful words?

"In seeking His desire for you in any situation, just recall what the Bible states, *We all stumble in many ways. Anyone who is never at fault in what they say is perfect, able to keep their whole body in check* [James 3:2 NIV]. Wow! Isn't that saying a lot? You see, although the tongue is a little member of your body, if you are willing to allow God to tame it, the rest of your body will follow. I am sure your experience has proven that this isn't something you can do on your own. The Epistle of James goes on to say, *The tongue also is a fire, a world of evil among the parts of the body. It corrupts the whole body, sets the whole course of one's life on fire, and is itself set on fire by hell* [James 3:6 NIV]."

Laura is thinking, *This is simply mind-boggling. I am particularly blown away by what she just stated, "Trials and tribulations will come along. Their purpose is to make you strong."* At this point, Laura is attempting to soak in everything that she is hearing. Her thirst for learning more about how to avoid confessing negativism really takes her by surprises.

Dr. Anderson is saying, "Talking about a mouthful, how many wars have been started by just the untamed tongue? Do your own words justify you, or do they condemn? Are you being blessed by your own words, or are you being cursed? Blessings and cursings proceed out of your mouth on a daily basis. You need to season your words carefully so that they don't hinder you or others. If you are constantly confessing negativism, you are your worst enemy! You need to solicit the help of the Holy Spirit to help tame your words. He stands ready to help you. Remember, in the Bible, Jesus tells us, *If ye love Me, keep My commandments. And I will pray the Father, and He shall give you another Comforter, that He may abide with you forever even the Spirit of truth whom the world cannot receive, because it seeth Him not, neither knoweth Him, but ye know Him, for He dwelleth with you, and shall be in you* [John 14:15–17 KJV]. Are you ready to lean in and listen to His Spirit?"

Dr. Anderson recognizes that the material covered is quite overwhelming for some attendees. So she offers them a ten-minute break.

Laura remains seated; her thoughts are all over the place.

Evidently, I am suffering from "information overload!" What happened to renewing my mind? Wait, that lesson was only about an hour ago. Guess those lessons need time to override so many years of negative thinking. It is going to take more than an hour for that "renewing my mind" lesson to kick in. Laura chuckles. *And oh my goodness, I never imagined the words coming out of my mouth could actually be doing me more harm than good*, thinks Laura.

7

After the break, Dr. Anderson grabs the attention of her audience by walking around the room and appearing to selectively look at specific attendees, nodding her head as if to say, "I get it. I know it is a lot to take in, but don't worry." It seems to be a unique strategy for "testing the emotional pulse" of her audience. Her smile is contagious. There is a comfortable silence in the room.

After a lengthy pause, Dr. Anderson continues, "Okay, I know you have received quite a bit of information this morning, and, yes, I know it can all be somewhat pretty daunting renewing your mind, unforgiveness, negative confessions, etc. Just remember, with the Holy Spirit's help, you are going to be okay. If you sincerely want to change, ask Him to help you, and He won't let you down. With God, all things are possible. You can change because *greater is He who is within you than he that is in the world* [1 John 4:4 KJV]. So don't look so downcast. Don't look so defeated. God has given you everything you need to say enough is enough to the battles that rage within you."

Wow! Laura makes a note that she just picked up another presentation strategy nugget. She simply found

Dr. Anderson's teaching style very effective at gaining the audience's attention.

Dr. Anderson continues, "I'll spend just a few more minutes talking about some of the other ugly spirits that we carry around in our intangible tank. All of these spirits feed off of each other. However, I don't want to end the seminar—focusing on intangible tank. This intangible tank stuff is bad news. It is clearly not something to dwell on. What I want you to dwell on is the good news! For the Bible is the good news, news that should be meditated on daily. So for every negative thought, I want you to counter it with something positive and what better way to do this than to immediately confess the Word of God. This is the only way you will be able to change your mindset, i.e., renew your mind."

After Dr. Anderson talks more about some of the other spirits contained in the intangible tank, she informs the attendees that further information on this subject can be found in her book, *The Battles Within: Enough Is Enough.*

She continues, "Having said that, I always like to end by introducing to some or reminding others about the importance of building a relationship with God through prayer. I want to ensure you understand the importance of prayer. Unfortunately, time won't allow me to adequately cover this topic. Therefore, I strongly encourage you to read more about prayer in chapter 1 ["A Model Prayer for All Times"] of my book. Each of you will be receiving a complimentary copy at the end of this seminar.

"Talking about praying. Let me pause and ask you this—have you asked yourself this question? 'Since our

Heavenly Father knows everything, which includes knowing the things we have need of, even before we ask Him, why should I pray at all?' Perhaps you have heard someone else say, 'What's the use of praying? Whatever is going to happen will happen anyway?'

"You should pray because God instructs you to do so. Yes, He knows all about you. Yes, He knows what you have need of before you pray. But simply put, you are to pray in obedience to His Word."

Dr. Anderson continues, "The Bible states, *Then Jesus told his disciples a parable to show them that they should always pray and not give up. He said, 'In a certain town, there was a judge who neither feared God nor cared what people thought. And there was a widow in that town who kept coming to him with the plea, "Grant me justice against my adversary." For some time, he refused. But finally, he said to himself, "Even though I don't fear God or care what people think, yet because this widow keeps bothering me, I will see that she gets justice, so that she won't eventually come and attack me!"' And the Lord said, 'Listen to what the unjust judge says. And will not God bring about justice for his chosen ones, who cry out to him day and night? Will he keep putting them off? I tell you, he will see that they get justice, and quickly. However, when the Son of Man comes, will he find faith on the earth?'* [Luke 18:1–7 NIV].

"Let's look at Matthew 6 where Jesus Himself is speaking, *And when you pray, do not be like the hypocrites, for they love to pray standing in the synagogues and on the street corners to be seen by others. Truly I tell you, they have received their reward in full. But when you pray, go into your room, close the door, and pray to your Father, who is unseen. Then your Father, who sees what is done in secret, will reward you. And when you pray, do not keep on babbling like pagans, for they think they will be heard because of their many words. Do not be like them, for your Father knows what you need before you ask him. This then is how you should pray—our Father in heaven, hallowed be your name, your kingdom come, your will be done, on earth as it is in heaven. Give us today our daily bread. And forgive us our debts, as we also have forgiven our debtors. And lead us not into temptation, but deliver us from the evil one* [Matthew 6:1–13 KJV].

"Please make a special note that although this text is referred to as 'The Lord's Prayer,' Jesus never prayed it Himself. Jesus gave this prayer to His disciples as a model to personalize their own prayers. When you pray, there's no need to use fancy words or lengthy opening remarks. There's no need to use deep, thought-provoking closing arguments. Prayer is a two-way conversation with the Father. You see, when you fully recognize that prayer involves having a personal relationship with God the Father through His Son, Jesus Christ, and that He is your everything, you will see the difference. When you recognize that He's not a faraway image, you will easily go to God in prayer just as a child goes to a parent. You will ask and believe that your Father has your best interest at heart.

"Our Father, Abba Father, this addresses God in a personal, intimate way. Always begin by praising Him and thanking Him for who He is. This delights our Father. I call this seeking the face of God, not the hand of God. When you read the chapter on prayer in my book, hopefully you will have a better understanding of the difference between seeking the face of God and seeking His hand.

"I highly recommend that you first create an atmosphere of praise for Him. Praise is bringing or offering up a sacrifice unto God, a sacrifice of praise. Our God, who has everything, has given us so many free gifts. So ask yourself this question—what can I give to God who has everything? How about a sacrifice of praise? This pleases our Father. You see, something happens in the spiritual world when you praise Him? Miracles will become evident in the physical world when you praise Him! It's important to create an atmosphere of praise for the Lord. The Bible tells us that God inhabits the praises of His people [Psalm 22:3 KJV]! When you get a hold of this, you are catching on to something awesome, something that words simply cannot describe!

"Now if you don't know God, you won't understand why it's so important to praise Him. There's no way you can know Him if you believe He is somewhere far out of reach. You see, the only way you will get to know God is through His Son, Jesus Christ. Listen to this, *Jesus saith unto him, I am the way, the truth, and the life. No man cometh unto the Father, but by me* [John 14:6 KJV]. So if you don't know His Son, you don't know Him. Listen to what Jesus says in Revelation 3:20, 'Behold, I stand at the door, and knock; if any man hears my voice, and open the door, I will come in to him, and will sup with him, and he with me.' So when you open the door and let Him come in, you will find that He's not out of reach.

"Because you are in a constant battle against sin and the devil, you need to rely on the Holy Spirit to help you resist temptation and overcome sin in your lives. When you ask God to 'deliver you from evil,' you are acknowledging that you don't have the power to do so on your own. You are acknowledging that you can do nothing without God's help. So you should seek God's help to overcome temptation and sin.

"Why pray? Because it is a way of communicating with the Heavenly Father. The other way you communicate with Him is by reading the Bible. More on both of these can be found in, yes, you guessed it, my book." And everyone laughs at Dr. Anderson's humor!

She concludes her brief presentation on prayer by quoting the Bible, *The Lord is nigh unto all them that call upon him, to all that call upon him, in truth. He will fulfill the desire of them that fear Him: He also will hear their cry, and will save them* (Psalm 145:18 KJV).

Dr. Anderson summarizes what was shared during today's two-hour seminar. She acknowledges that time only allowed her to merely touch the surface. She then reminds everyone to keep notes in their daily journals as an excellent step in staying focused on their path to a life that is God pleasing, a life that is abundant and meaningful.

She distributes complimentary copies of her book, *The Battles Within: Enough Is Enough*, to all attendees. Finally, she concludes the seminar in prayer, asking God to provide wisdom and protection to each of them. Then she bids them farewell.

The seminar ends around 11:30 a.m., and shortly afterward, Tina approaches Laura and lets her know that she is, indeed, available to meet with her over dinner later. They exchange contact information and agree to meet in the hotel lobby at 6:45 p.m. Laura couldn't understand how she could feel both emotionally drained and exuberated at the same time.

"Wow! What a great seminar!" she exclaims to no one in particular.

After picking up her autographed copy of Dr. Anderson's book, she exchanges a few comments with other attendees and finally returns to her hotel.

Who could have convinced me yesterday that I would be here today, having just sat through a very eye-opening two-hour Christian seminar?

8

Back at her hotel, Laura grabs a sandwich, a bag of chips, and a coke before heading upstairs to relax in her room. She immediately checks her cell phone to see if she had received any urgent calls; she had deliberately turned it off earlier that morning. After confirming there are none, she eats lunch while going over some of her notes from the seminar. She had already decided against checking her home phone voice mail for fear she may have received more disturbing calls. Before leaving home, she had chosen not to forward her home phone number to her cell phone. She admits being a little disappointed that Drew hadn't called her, even though she had left him a message concerning her whereabouts. For now, she doesn't want to focus on these or any other distractions.

After suffering from sleep deprivation for over a month now, Laura hopes to catch a nap (without the aid of sleeping pills) before meeting Tina. Not wanting to be late for dinner, she sets the alarm just in case sleep does come. With so many thoughts swirling through her mind, she's having difficulty mentally turning off snippets of seminar information. She plans to send a thank-you note to Dr. Anderson; she also makes a note to purchase a journal as was highly recommended. She feels the need to check in with her sons as it's been a few days since chatting with any of them.

So many things to do, thinks Laura.

Finally overcome by exhaustion, sleep beckons her, and she doses off for a few minutes. She is startled awake by the ringing of the hotel phone, fire alarms going off, and lots of commotion in the hallway outside her room—all happening at the same time. Somewhat disoriented by being abruptly awakened and in unfamiliar surroundings, Laura quickly jumps up, grabs her phone, and along with other hysterical guests, races to the nearest fire exit.

Outside the hotel where guests are gathering, smelling no smoke, everyone is frantically trying to find out what could possibly be going on. A false alarm? A fire drill? After about twenty minutes, they get the all-clear and mumbling guests are allowed to return to their hotel rooms. Catching her breath as she goes to unlock the door to her room, Laura notices that it is ajar and unexpectedly has a sickening feeling that something is not quite right. She frantically looks up and down the hall. Then without thinking, she rushes into her room and straightway observes that it has clearly been ransacked. Her clothing and contents from her purse are all strewn on the floor.

She remembers slamming the door behind her when she left due to the fire alarm. Alarmed, she immediately backs out of her room and uses her cell phone to call the front desk.

Hotel security team arrive to find a very frightened Laura standing outside her room, near her door. After greeting her, the security team enters the room and does a thorough inspection, including dusting for fingerprints. They ask her to make a list of any missing items. As they stand watch, she checks around her room.

Then she says, "There doesn't appear to be anything missing."

The security team steps into the hallway to exchange information among themselves. After checking in with hotel management, they compare notes and determine that Laura's ransacked room is the only reported case. Obviously, this leaves them with more concerns.

Although they don't want to alarm her any more than necessary, the security team determines that a more thorough investigation is warranted and proceeds to ask her some personal questions.

She doesn't say anything to them regarding her encounter with the stranger, but she does mention the recurring "hang-up" phone calls. They advise her to contact the local authorities regarding the phone calls as soon as possible. She makes a commitment to do so. She answers most of their questions and later adds that she fears she may have either been followed or watched while in and near the hotel premises. They take special note of this information and promise to review the hotel camera footage and take any other appropriate actions, etc.

In the meantime, Laura's thoughts are working overtime. *Is this personal? If so, how does anyone know I am here, except Drew, and, oh, by the way, why haven't I even heard from him? I've left him several messages! Was this break-in somehow connected to the stranger's news or the recurring phone calls? Was it somehow connected to anyone I may have encountered at the seminar? Was someone actually following or watching me? Why? Oh, for crying out loud, am I being overly suspicious?*

It is now 5:00 p.m., and the security team has finally left, promising to follow up with her later. After all the flurry of activities, which includes being reassigned to a different hotel room, Laura's thoughts eventually turn to her 7:00 p.m. dinner meeting with Tina, which had completely slipped her mind. She calls her to let her know what has happened, and that perhaps they should cancel their dinner plans. Tina has a better idea; she really doesn't want Laura to be alone.

"Why not come to my suite now, and we can dine in and chat?" she offers.

Laura initially hesitates, then gratefully accepts her invitation. Not really wanting to be alone, she breathes a sign of relief as she grabs her purse, seminar notes, and Dr. Anderson's book. She makes a point of double-checking to ensure her door is locked, then glances up and down the hallway before heading for the elevator.

9

Tina greets Laura and warmly welcomes her into her suite. Quickly observing how distraught Laura appears to be, she gives her a hug and tries to reassure her new friend that the hotel will get to the bottom of this mess. Tina does not understand that the ransacked room is but one of many issues burdening Laura at this time. Once seated, she pours each of them a cup of tea, and they just sit quietly for a couple of minutes, each absorbed in her own thoughts, silently reflecting on the day's events.

After a few minutes of silence, Tina asks her if she wants to get the dinner orders out of the way, so they can relax and become better acquainted. Laura agrees, and their selections are placed. Dinner is expected to arrive in about one hour.

They continue to sit in silence. Tina is inwardly praying and asking God for guidance on how to best proceed in gaining Laura's trust so she can help her. Laura is trying to decide just how much information she can entrust to her. She still has mixed emotions. So she elects not to mention her encounter with the stranger or the recurring "hang-up" phone calls.

She's thinking, *After all, how much do I really know about her? Why is she being so friendly toward me? Can I fully trust her as I assumed earlier? If not her, who can I trust? Was our meeting coincidental or something God planned? God, I really do need a friend. Please show me a sign.* She pleads inwardly.

After about five more minutes, Tina senses a green light from the Holy Spirit and breaks their silence by asking Laura if she is comfortable with joining her in prayer. Laura timidly agrees, and she proceeds.

"Dear Heavenly Father. We thank You for being such a wonderful Father and always knowing and supplying our every need. While we don't always know what to pray or do, we know You do. We know we can't go wrong when we align our prayer with Your Word. *So we come boldly to you, praying with sincere hearts, 'Our Father in heaven, hallowed be your name, your kingdom come, your will be done, on earth as it is in heaven. Give us today our daily bread. And forgive us our debts, as we also have forgiven our debtors. And lead us not into temptation, but deliver us from the evil one'* [Matthew 6:9–16 NIV].

"Father, I also thank You for Laura and for what You are going to do through this friendship. We ask for Your guidance and Your continued wisdom as we cross unchartered territories. In Your Son Jesus's Name, we pray. Amen."

Although still nervous about her room being invaded and not knowing whether it is anyway connected to the other recent issues in her life, Laura finds the prayer to be comforting and starts to relax a little. Taking a sip of her tea, she senses such a peaceful atmosphere and silently thanks God for bringing Tina into her life as well.

Tina begins their discussion by telling Laura a little more about herself.

"As I mentioned to you during the seminar, I work at Dr. Anderson's firm as a psychologist. We initially met at a convention about five years ago and quickly realized we had a lot in common. For one thing, we were both widowed about two years before we met. Dr. Anderson has commonly shared her experiences as a widow, so that's not a secret. Shortly after that, I started working at her firm and eventually was promoted to an associate partner position. Working with Dr. Anderson has been so rewarding. I've learned so much from her and will always be grateful for how she takes the time to help me on my Christian journey. When I am not extremely busy at the firm, I occasionally travel with her and provide assistance during her seminars as needed. It doesn't matter how many times I've heard her speak on various topics, I always pick up some useful information that helps me develop, whether in my professional life or on a personal basis.

"Speaking of which, I really enjoyed her seminar today. She is a very sought-after speaker, and this particular seminar, *The Battles Within: Enough Is Enough* was selected among hundreds of other seminar topics (by various speakers) to be included in this annual conference. This conference, which is scheduled for one full week, includes four other seminars, taught by other speakers. However, registrations for Dr. Anderson's seminars always tend to fill up quickly. I am not sure when you registered for it, but it is a good thing that you were able to get in."

If this is true, I found it very interesting that I was able to actually get a space. I only registered yesterday, thinks Laura.

She continues, "Laura, trust me on this—you can tell me as little or as much about yourself as you are comfortable sharing. I have no hidden agenda. I believe the Lord orchestrated our meeting each other earlier today. As I mentioned when we first met, this meeting is not on a professional level, yet anything you elect to share with me will be kept on a confidential basis."

She pauses to give Laura an opportunity to chime in. Laura is being reserved in what she shares. So her response is still a little guarded as she chimes in.

"Tina, once again, I want to thank you for being there for me during the seminar this morning and now especially with all that just happened with my room being invaded. You have got to be wondering what in the world possessed you to come to my aid! No doubt, if I were you, I'd probably be wondering the same thing. This may sound comical, but there's no doubt in my mind that if you hadn't come to my rescue during the seminar this morning, someone probably would have come to take me out of that room on a stretcher! As I am sure you saw, I was simply a basket case and had a really difficult time keeping it all together. There is so much happening in my life right now. Most of it, I am just not prepared to talk about. I will tell you this. Listening to Dr. Anderson delve into so many important topics so close to home really stirred up something within me. It was like she was reading my mind and tapping into my every thought! It was like she was speaking directly to me, and I was asking myself, 'Is my life such an open book?'

"Even though I accepted Jesus as my personal Savior a long time ago, I haven't lived a life that I know is pleasing to Him. If I am to be completely honest, I'll tell you something else. A lot of what Dr. Anderson talked about when she referred to the Holy Spirit as our comforter, our helper, our guide was really foreign to me. I am ashamed to admit, but I haven't been an earnest Bible student. So listening to her talk about those things has caused me to do some serious thinking. It has caused me to reevaluate my priorities. It has caused me to want to learn more about many of the topics she shared today."

Tina smiles and says, "I completely understand what you are saying. However, let me first say this. Based on my experience and what some of the other attendees shared with me, I can promise you, Dr. Anderson was not reading your mind, but God was. You see, because each of us are so uniquely important to God, our life is an open book to Him, and get this, we are always on His mind. Laura, you see, the Holy Spirit knows exactly what each of us need. He will do whatever He needs to do whenever and however He needs to do it to get our attention. He wants the best for us, and because He knows the road we are traveling, He allows special people to cross our paths to help us stay on track. I don't want to come across as continually singing the praises of Dr. Anderson [because all praises should certainly go to God], but she is definitely one of those special people who God has chosen to help us live victorious lives.

"Over the years, I have watched how she prepares for each of her seminars. I've seen and heard her pray before each seminar, asking God for wisdom and direction. While she rarely knows anything about the attendees' personal lives, she certainly acknowledges that God does know. She relies heavily on Him for guidance concerning her presentation topics. She also asks God to prepare the hearts of the attendees so they are open to receive everything that He intends for them. Dr. Anderson relies on Jeremiah 29:11, *"For I know the plans I have for you, says the Lord. They are plans for good and not for evil, to give you a future and a hope."*

"Now speaking of today's seminar, tell me, did you find the seminar interesting? Any particular takeaways?"

Laura had listened intently to what she was sharing about Dr. Anderson, particularly how she approached God in prayer for direction. She really wanted to learn more about doing that and relying heavily on the Holy Spirit for wisdom and guidance. Inwardly, she was asking God for some type of direction on what to share with her.

She thought this was an excellent segue to discuss something that was foremost on her mind. Actually, it was the main reason she had asked Tina to meet with her. However, she thought it only fair that since Tina had opened up a little about her background, she should do the same. Of course, she plans to stay on safe grounds.

"Yes, but before we talk about takeaways from the seminar, I'd like to tell you a little about myself."

10

"I've been an English professor at Chestnut-Patterson University for about five years. Up until recently, I enjoyed teaching. I actually found it fulfilling. However, due to some serious personal matters, I am currently taking a leave of absence from work. This is what led me to come to this resort. However, I had no idea when I came here that I would actually end up attending any type of seminar! Coincident or divine intervention? Whichever, I am glad I came.

"I am forty-seven years old and have been married for about twenty-four years. I have three adult sons.

"Now to answer your question, yes, I truly enjoyed the seminar and am still attempting to digest much of what I learned today. The subject of unforgiveness has particularly been tugging at me for quite some time. So I found that lesson to clearly be one of my most needed takeaways. The fire alarm actually woke me up from a much-needed nap."

Thinking about the fire alarm episode, Laura frowns, then continues, "Before my nap, I had actually been thinking about what I learned from the seminar and how interesting it was that I was able to temporarily put my other issues—and there are so many—on the back burner. Also, the subject of approaching God in prayer has definitely become more urgent."

Watching Tina and believing that she sincerely wants to hear more about what's on her mind, Laura continues, "Earlier this afternoon, I heard an inner sweet gentle voice gently reminding me of the importance of forgiving before moving forward. This inner prompting took me back to something Dr. Anderson mentioned during the seminar. She stated, '*Let's begin with unforgiveness. Yes, I believe this one should be at the top of our list as it alone holds the key to so many issues. Have you forgiven yourself or others for past actions?*'

"Tina, I am so tired of feeling guilty for something I did years ago. I know I need to get rid of the feelings of pains and disappointments from my past. I truly want to begin the healing process of pushing past this pain so I can move forward with confidence toward the purpose God has planned for me. I really desire God's guidance right now."

Laura becomes silent as if waiting for a clue to continue. Tina remains silent. There is complete silence in the room. She is aware that the Holy Spirit is about to perform surgery in Laura's life, and she does not want to interfere with that process.

Not fully understanding that God, an ever-present God, is indeed listening to her at this very moment, Laura cries, "Lord, help me to get this out in the open, for I am tired of carrying this burden alone." Suddenly, she starts to weep as memories of that awful night, and the painful weeks that followed flood her mind.

She offers Laura a glass of water. After taking a sip, Laura pauses and moves from the chair to a comfortable position on the floor, supporting her back with a couple of pillows. Then Laura proceeds to share her long-kept secret with her new friend, finally believing that she will not judge her as she has judged herself.

"I literally feel like I am traveling back in time to the most awful night of my life. It is late autumn, on a Friday night, and I am in my freshman year at Williams & McIntire University. You see, I thought I had it all together. I was nineteen then and considered myself 'grown!' I wanted to cast aside some of those lessons that my precious Mama had tried to instill in me since childhood. Mama was always talking and preaching about what not to do. I was now in college and doing my own thing. So that night after an off-campus party, I was trying hard to silence Mama's voice. Against my better judgment, I let this jockey junior guy into my room. You see, we had started a conversation at the party, and because the place was packed and very loud, this guy had suggested that we go to my dorm room so we could have a quieter place to continue chatting. I knew my dorm mate was away for the weekend. That should have been a red flag of just how stupid I was acting! Well, in hindsight, I should have listened to those alarm bells going on in my head, but I agreed with him. Shortly, we left the party together. I was feeling like a big girl, thinking, *No big deal. I can handle this. All we are going to do is chat and maybe some occasional necking.*

"Yes, that was all I had planned to do. I never intended more. I never wanted more. After all, I was still a virgin and had always planned to walk down the aisle as one to marry the man of my dreams and, as the saying goes, live happily ever after. Sure, I had been teased by my girlfriends for maintaining my virginity. However, I had held fast to my pledge.

"But this guy who will remain nameless, this guy who was on the football team, this guy who I had literally just met through one of our mutual friends, this guy, this jockey wasn't playing that 'all I want to do is talk and neck.' Little did I know, he had much more on his mind and absolutely wasn't planning to take no for an answer. In his mind, getting what he wanted from this silly country girl would be just another notch on his belt.

"After we entered my dorm room, this guy immediately locked the door behind us and began tugging on my clothing. He didn't even give me a chance to question what he was doing. I was shouting, 'What are you doing? No, no, no' over and over and over again. But this guy must have thought I was merely teasing him. Tina, I really tried to resist him. I tried so hard to physically fight him off, but he was so much stronger than I was.

"Oh, Tina, it is all coming back to me now, my silent screams, my clawing at him, and my shutting my eyes tight. I was wishing it was all just a terrible, terrible dream. I tried to cry out more, but he prevented me from doing so by putting one hand over my mouth. I tried to bite his hand, but he slapped me. He actually slapped me. I could smell the alcohol on his breath, and before I could stop him, he took full advantage of me. Yes, me, this girl from Chapel Hill, who previously thought I had it all together.

He brutally took my innocence, and then as quickly as he had entered my room, he left, leaving me in physical agony and pain. I was feeling ashamed, humiliated, and totally defeated.

"Tina, oh my goodness! I stayed in my dorm room all that weekend, just hugging myself, trembling, crying, and wishing I could crawl into some dark pit and die literally. You know, I never reported the incident to the campus police, for I didn't think anyone would believe I was an unwilling participant. I never said anything to my dorm mate when she returned from out of town that Sunday night. I never said anything to anyone! Why didn't I? Oh my god! Why didn't I? I've often wondered if I had reported this incident, may be things would have turned out differently. If I had reported this incident, perhaps I might have saved some other innocent girl from a life of shame. Regardless, I will never know now, will I?

"I was this country girl from Chapel Hill who blamed myself. I was convinced in my own little world that it was all my fault simply because I had started the whole thing by flirting with this popular football player. I never heard from him again. He would see me around campus and pretend he had never met me. I avoided him as much as possible as well. I hated him. I actually hated him, but get this, I hated myself even more!

"Tina, my dear friend, this story doesn't end here though. Oh, how I wished it did!"

By this time, Laura is so overwhelmed with tears; she's shaking uncontrollably but eventually manages to continue her story.

"About five weeks later, my biggest fear was confirmed. Yes, you guessed it! I began to feel ill, especially in the mornings. I finally took a home pregnancy test and learned I was pregnant. I was pregnant by someone who never loved me. I was pregnant by someone I didn't even know and definitely didn't love! I was pregnant by someone who brutally took advantage of my innocence! I was pregnant by someone who I actually despised! I remembered thinking, 'This naive little country girl from Chapel Hill has gotten herself into the worst predicament imaginable.' I was too ashamed to even call my dear mama.

"Talking about feelings of guilt and tremendous shame, then believing I had no one to talk with, no one who cared, nowhere to turn, I did what I now so dreadfully regret. That's right, me, this girl from Chapel Hill, who thought I had it all together. I gave in to the one thing that has haunted me ever since. Feeling all alone and hopeless, I borrowed money from a couple of friends and went to a clinic. Lying on the table with no one to comfort me, no one to hold my hand, no one to convince me that this really wasn't the way to go, I simply couldn't believe what was happening. Even then, at that very moment, I didn't believe I had any options. I began to shake uncontrollably. In my heart, I knew I was about to do something that would change my life forever. Yet I willed myself to remain still. It was like I was having an out-of-body experience. I forced my mind to just shut off, to go to a place that was far, far away from that awful small filthy-smelling room. I willed myself to ignore all of the warning bells going off in my head and finally, finally, gave in! What must I have been thinking? Yes, I aborted my precious, precious inno-cent baby."

Silence, except for Laura's occasional moans and snif-fles, during which time, Tina hands her some tissues. The room is silent. Neither she nor Laura speaks. With tears flowing down her face, Laura looks at Tina. She stares back at Laura. No judging stare, just one out of genuine com-passion. There's the ticktock sounds of a clock somewhere off in the distance, but both remain speechless. She sus-pects there is more to Laura's story, so she doesn't move. She doesn't make a sound. She wants to go to Laura, but something within her stops her, something within her tells her to hold off. That now is not the right time. Instead, she senses now is the time for her to pray and wait patiently.

The waiter's knock on the door breaks the silence, causing Tina to answer and retrieve the ordered dinner. She quietly closes the door and places the food in the kitchen-ette. She quickly returns to where a moaning Laura is still crouching on the floor. Neither is thinking about eating right now. Finally, Laura takes a deep breath and a sip of water, looks up at Tina with tears still flowing down her face, and continues.

"Now I have recurring nightmares that won't let me rest. They always get more frequent during this time of the year, autumn season. In my dreams, I keep hearing a little girl crying out in the middle of the night. You may be asking how do I know it's a little girl's voice? After all, don't all babies' cries sound the same? I can't answer that, but I feel deep down in my heart that it is a little girl's cry. Trust me, I've asked myself this very question so many times. At any rate in my dreams, I follow that voice. I try to get to her, but I can't. Her voice keeps getting farther away, fainter and fainter until I can't hear it anymore. It is such a desperate, sad voice. Then I wake up, exhausted. And you want to know what is the most sorrowful and confusing part of it all? I can't figure out whether it is my aborted baby crying out to me or if it is my own innocence that was taken, crying out to my mama. There is a difference. There must be a difference. Even though they are interrelated, please tell me, there is a difference, right?

"Oh my goodness, I miss my mama. Oh my goodness! I wish I could rock and hold my baby and let her know just how truly sorry I am. Regardless, I wish I hadn't aborted my baby! I wish I had had the strength to go home to Mama. Thinking back, I don't believe Mama would have judged me. I don't believe Mama would have despised or hated me. Maybe it's because I didn't want to disappoint her. I believe she would have loved me no matter what. Why didn't I just go to her? Oh my goodness, what am I supposed to do now? Mama's gone, my baby's gone, and here I am, left with this sickening, empty feeling even after all these years."

Tina still doesn't move. She has her head bowed low. She's silently praying, asking God for guidance.

Laura continues to cry out, and then looking totally astonished, she desperately hollers out, "Tina, oh my goodness, did I just tell you all of that? Oh my goodness, I've never told anyone this story, not even my husband. Can you believe that? What in the world possessed me to tell you all of this? I am so ashamed! After all these years, I've carried this dark shameful secret with me. I don't know what to do about it now."

Laura is hysterical. Tina is still inwardly praying.

Tina finally lowers herself from where she is sitting in a chair to the place where Laura is still crouching on the floor and gently begins to cradle her. She can't help herself and starts softly crying alongside Laura. She just lets her cry and cry and cry.

Afterward, Laura catches her breath and helplessly stares at Tina and asks, "Will God still love someone like me, someone as awful as me? Will He ever forgive me for that awful, fateful night? Will God ever forgive me for aborting my precious baby? Will God ever forgive me for hating that football player, that boy with no name? Will I ever be able to look at someone's baby girl and not want to run away and hide? Can you tell me whether the forgiveness that Dr. Anderson talked so much about during the seminar extends to me as well?"

Tina senses in her spirit that this is the time for Laura's healing. This is the time for God to perform His surgery in Laura's heart. By this time, she finds herself trying desperately to stop her own tears as she continues to inwardly pray for God to take the wheel!

After what seems like a lengthy pause, she looks at Laura and says, "Now is the time. Now we can pray. Now we should pray, and you can once and for all release this burden totally to God. This burden wasn't meant for you to carry. You see, my dear friend, God hears you and sees your tears. He feels your pain. He's always felt your pain. He was just waiting for you to come to Him. We can now pray, and, yes, God can and will forgive you. Forgiveness is yours for the asking. Get this, Laura, God loves you so unconditionally. Do you believe this? There is nothing you can do that will cause God to love you less? The Bible tells us in Romans 8:29, *Neither height nor depth, nor anything else in all creation, will be able to separate us from the love of God that is in Christ Jesus, our Lord.* Do you believe that, my dear friend?

"Just sit here and talk to God like you just talked to me. He's listening. I want you to talk to God. That's praying, and I'll just be nearby, praying, interceding for you. I feel the need to step aside and let you have your time with God. This should be your moment with Him, but get this—I am not going anywhere. Know this, I am here for you. I'll just be nearby in the other room if you need me."

11

Laura, the girl from Chapel Hill, finally resolves to cast this particular burden over to the Lord once and for all. She's thinking about something Tina just said, "Just sit here and talk to God like you just talked to me." She knows she has a lot to learn about approaching God in prayer, but she also knows she has to start somewhere. So she begins to simply talk to Him, clinging to His Word as best as she knows how by just saying what's on her heart.

"Lord, I need You now. Lord, I just want to rest. I need Your forgiveness. Lord, help me to forgive myself. Lord, please help me love myself. Lord, help me to forgive that nameless jockey boy who took advantage of my innocence. Lord, I need You now!"

Yes, Laura is praying to God, and, yes, He is indeed listening. For as always, He holds her ever so gently even more so than a mother holds her own child who is deeply hurting.

With tears continuing to flow, Laura is down on her knees and suddenly feels an urge to read some familiar Bible passages. She recalls that hotels customarily keep a Bible in the guest rooms even though nowadays, most people can access it via their cell phones. So she quietly calls out to Tina and asks that she check her nightstand for a Bible. Tina opens her bedside nightstand drawer and, lo and behold, finds such a welcoming sight, a print copy of a Bible. She quickly hands it over to Laura, not saying a word.

Browsing through her notes from the seminar and Dr. Anderson's book, Laura locates the referenced Scriptures on forgiveness. She then researches them in the Bible she is now holding in her hands. As she stares down at the Bible, warm and familiar emotions stir within her, awakening sweet vivid memories of Mama and her old torn Bible.

She quickly reads, *For if ye forgive men their trespasses, your heavenly Father will also forgive you: But if ye forgive not men their trespasses, neither will your Father forgive your trespasses* (Matthew 6:14–15 KJV).

"Dear Heavenly Father, I know I don't have this all together yet. But here I am—as raw as they come. I am tired of beating up on myself for my past sins. I am tired of fighting these battles within. I know I accepted You as my Savior when I was little many years ago, but I've drifted so far away from Your teachings. I've drifted so far away from what Mama taught me. I finally realize I don't want to rely on Mama's faith anymore. I want to rely on my own. I acknowledge that I can only do this with Your strength. Father, I know I've made a mess of things, but please hear my cry. All my life, I've tried to do this on my own. I'm weak, but I know You are strong. Please help me to forgive that boy for what he did to me all those many years ago. Please remove the bitterness and hatred that I feel for him from my heart and replace it with a spirit of forgiveness.

Father, I ask that You, please forgive me for aborting my precious baby and please keep her in Your loving arms. For one day, I want to meet her and tell her how much I love her. Lord, I am sincerely sorry for all of this and for any other sins I've ever committed through thought, word, or deed."

Taking a deep breath, Laura pauses and smiles through her tears. She continues, "Father thank You for loving me even when I didn't love myself. Thank You for cleansing me as only You can. Father, I know there are so many other things I probably should say, but for now, I hope I got this right. Oh, and before I forget, Father, thank You for sending Tina my way. Yes, according to Your Word, I believe I got this right. In Jesus's name. Amen!"

Laura remains on her knees for a few minutes, breathing in a deep sigh of relief as she becomes enveloped by an overwhelming sense of warmth, comfort, and peace. Something wonderful has just happened to her. She has finally let go of the burden she carried all these years. She has finally laid it at the feet of Jesus. She has just experienced the most wonderful cleansing power of forgiveness. This is something she will cherish forever, knowing forever is a very long time!

Getting up off the floor, Laura looks around. She knows her physical environment is the same, but somehow, somewhere deep within, she feels different. She knows it is a spiritual awakening. She smiles, she laughs, she sheds more tears, but the difference is—these are tears of joy. She is so thankful to God for never letting go of her, even when she wanted to let go of it all. She's thankful that although she felt she was at the end of the rope, she was able to tie a knot and hang on. She knows this is not of her own strength. She knows God has purged something within her. There are still a lot of things she doesn't know, but she knows that God was there for her when she felt helpless. She also knows that God put Tina in her life for such a time as this.

She doesn't know about tomorrow; she doesn't know how the other traumatic issues in her life are going to end. But for now, for tonight, for this moment, she's confident that the little girl has stopped crying. She's confident and free of this burden. She's confident that her beautiful baby is finally at rest.

Laura finally calls out to Tina, who enters the room and smiles. They hug, look at each other, look up to God, and hug some more.

Then because no other words are needed at this time, Tina simply says, "Let's eat dinner."

Laura replies, "Sounds good. I am starved!"

They both start laughing.

During dinnertime, they exchange more notes from Dr. Anderson's seminar. Laura asks Tina to explain several Scriptures that were referenced during the seminar, and she happily obliges. She's excited to help a fellow student in her new quest for spiritual development. She opens up more about her own journey of faith and how others have helped her overcome several challenges. She encourages Laura by saying, "None of us are perfect. We all make mistakes. I have got a long way to go. But one thing I can be sure of, I will never, ever be alone. Neither will you, for God promises to always be with us."

Dinnertime is a comfortable moment shared by two new friends who both feel as if they've been knowing each other for years.

After dinner, Laura announces she's leaving to return to her hotel room. Tina suggests Laura spend the night in her suite, but Laura insists on returning to her own room. However, sensing Tina's concern for her safety, Laura holds up her cell phone and says, "Let's chat on the phone until I am safely in my room."

"Sounds like a plan," agrees Tina as she walks Laura to the door and keeps watch until she gets to the elevator.

Laura peeps inside the elevator and sends her a "thumbs-up," signifying that all is well. Inwardly, Tina continues to pray for Laura's protection.

Safely back in her room, Laura says good night to Tina on the cell phone. She then double-checks her door locks and takes her shower. Even though she's a little worn-out, she proceeds to read a bit from the nightstand Bible. Then finally overcome by exhaustion, sleep beckons her, and her body finally succumbs to a very welcoming state of oblivion.

12

Laura awakens before the alarm goes off and is pleasantly surprised to feel rested from an uneventful sleep. It dawns on her that she didn't even take any sleeping pills last night. Amazingly refreshed, she begins to plan her day.

She calls Tina and thanks her again for everything. Tina mentions that she's heading over to the conference. She will be assisting Dr. Anderson at another session today. She shares with Laura that one of her favorite Scriptures to meditate on when she's feeling anxious or worry is, *Do not be anxious about anything, but in every situation, by prayer and petition, with thanksgiving, present your requests to God* (Philippians 4:6 NIV).

"Sounds like a wonderful idea," Laura agrees. "I will definitely set aside some time today and meditate on this one."

Before hanging up, the two promise to keep in touch.

After grabbing a breakfast sandwich and tea from the hotel cafe, Laura stops by the gift shop and purchases a journal, per Dr. Anderson's recommendation. She is anxious to record in her journal, especially how she applies the "intangible tank" lessons learned during the seminar. She also plans to record the freedom she now experiences after last night's deliverance.

While Laura is definitely experiencing freedom from past feelings of guilt and pain, her mind now turns to the shocking news from the stranger. Reality is setting in that she will be hearing from him soon. She would be fooling herself if she didn't admit that her encounter with the stranger still troubles her. She recalls he instructed her not to say anything about their meeting to anyone. However, since he didn't give her a chance to respond, she didn't commit to that. So she's pondering whether to share it with Tina and, more importantly, the security officer.

Laura returns to her room to catch up on some reading. She tries to reach Drew again but still no success. What would she say to him when they finally chatted? Would she reveal the secret she had kept hidden all these years? Would he think badly of her? Would he forgive her for not opening up that part of her life to him? Would he understand and rejoice with her that she is truly free from her past pains now? And what about the stranger's news? Since Drew had been so distant lately, Laura wasn't sure if she could even trust him with her true feelings about anything.

Last night during dinner, Tina had encouraged her to start her day off with devotions. Initially, her devotions included a repeat of what was commonly called "The Lord's Prayer." With the sweet memory of her deliverance in Tina's room last night, she now personalizes her prayer by thanking God for releasing her from the guilt of her past. She thanks Him for forgiving her and for giving her the strength to forgive that football player. Thanks to God, she can now think of that night without feeling the sting of pain and loss. She is so grateful and finds it amazing how the Holy Spirit freed her from the burden of her past. Although she is currently facing other frightening ordeals, she has the reassurance that God will never leave her. Yes, she still wrestles with some anxiety of the unknown but is determined to walk more by faith and not by sight.

"God, please help me on my faith journey," Laura prays.

Suddenly realizing that she had forgotten to turn up the ring volume on her cell phone when she woke up this morning, she checks it quickly. There was a voice mail message from Anne, one of her colleagues at the university, asking her to return the call as soon as possible. She thought that was strange as the two of them rarely spoke, but Anne was one of the few people who Laura had exchanged contact information. The two had occasionally met for lunch. Perhaps her call was in reference to Laura's classroom as Anne has occasionally filled in for her as a substitute. There was a missed call from her son Mike, but as usual, he didn't leave a message.

Probably asking for some money, thinks Laura, shaking her head. "He really has a problem managing his allowance and knows he'll get his way with me, but not his dad. That's my baby." Laura smiles.

Looking at the clock, Laura realizes Mike's still in class, so she plans to return his call later.

Laura returns the call to Anne, but no answer. So she leaves her a message.

While waiting for Anne to call again, Laura reviews some of her notes from yesterday's seminar and decides to read a chapter or two from Dr. Anderson's book. Randomly flipping through the book, her eyes immediately land on chapter 4 ("Are You Operating in Fear or Faith?"). Interesting. For some reason, some of this information seems to be drawing her in, almost like a magnet. Little did Laura know that within the hour, she would be clinging to this information as if her life depended on it.

Lying across the bed, Laura gets comfortable and starts reading chapter 4.

"Are you operating in fear or faith? What are you allowing to control you? From Genesis to Revelation, the Word of God admonishes us to cast away fear. I know from personal experience that fear will paralyze you, and when this happens, you can't focus. You feel like you are stuck in a no-win situation. We all know what fear is, we know how it makes us feel, we know how it makes us think, and we know how it makes us behave. Where does fear come from? The Bible states *that God did not give us the spirit of fear, but of love, of power and of a sound mind* [2 Timothy 1:7 KJV]. So please understand this—the spirit of fear does not come from God.

"So what is faith? The Bible says, *Now faith is the substance of things hoped for; the evidence of things not seen* [Hebrews 11:1 KJV]. Are you operating in fear or faith? What motivates you in every situation? Spiritually, fear is a trick of the enemy, an entrapment to keep you from trusting in God. Fear is a snarl, a trap to cause you to take your eyes off God and stay focused on the problem. Fear is a serious tool used by the enemy to keep you in bondage. Fear paralyzes you and keeps you from moving forward. Faith propels you and positions you to receive with joy all that He has for you. Fear is failure to progress. Faith is hope in action!

"From Genesis to Revelation, we find examples throughout the Bible where God first told His people to 'fear not' before He told them anything else. For God knew that the spirit of fear needed to be conquered before man could trust and depend on Him. He knew the spirit of fear needed to be conquered before man could go to the next level. God knew the spirit of fear needed to be conquered before man's mind could be renewed. So God, being a God of order, first instructs man to 'fear not.' God knew what that awful spirit of fear would do to man. He knew it because He knew the very spirit from which it came. God knew that the spirit of fear didn't come from Him. All throughout the Word of God, from Genesis to Revelation, He instructed man to cast away fear.

"Get this—you have got to get rid of this fear in order to let God be God in your life. You can't allow your circumstances to control you. You can't allow your situation—what it looks like—to determine the outcome. You are currently looking through a glass dimly. So you can't see the entire picture, but God does!

"Oftentimes fear shows up as a reminder of your past to get you to take your eyes off God, to get you to focus on the problem, not the promise. And understand this—your past does not determine your future. Stop looking back at what you consider to be past failures and stop allowing your past to dictate your future.

"We are talking about a God who didn't create fear. Yet He created opportunities for us to trust Him when fear threatens to overtake us. We are talking about a God who didn't give us a spirit of fear, yet even in the midst of a fearful situation, He creates a way for us to escape by trusting Him."

Something nudges Laura's memory. *Wasn't I just thinking about how to walk more by faith and not by sight? Is this a coincidence that I am now reading about fear versus faith?* thinks Laura as she continues her reading.

"From the beginning of time, flesh has caused man to operate in fear. From Genesis to Revelation, flesh has caused man to mess up. From Genesis to Revelation, flesh has cause man to miss his blessings, yet God admonishes man throughout all time to fear not!

"Flesh will cause you to yield to temptation. It tempts you to doubt God. It tempts you to do things your way. It tempts you to take your focus off God and see the problem instead of trusting that God knows what He is doing. When we walk in the Spirit, we walk according to faith and not by sight.

"Do you know that the five senses will cause you to embrace the spirit of fear, instead of the spiritual senses [the fruit of His Spirit]? If you are led by the Spirit, you will crucify the flesh. If you are led by the Spirit, you will allow His wonderful fruit to enable you to embrace faith. If you are led by the Spirit, you will only do those things that please

Him. The flesh desires us to be fearful. The Spirit desires us to be faithful.

"The flesh desires us to be doubtful. The Spirit desires us to be trusting. The flesh desires us to be wavering. The Spirit desires us to be steadfast. Please understand this— the flesh desires us to lean to our own understanding. The Spirit desires us to see those things that are not as though they are. So, my friend, are you operating in fear or faith?"

Laura is so engrossed in this chapter that the ringing of the hotel phone startles her. Upon answering it, she learns the caller is the hotel security officer. He asks Laura to come down to the security office and review some camera footage. Agreeing to do so, Laura becomes anxious and finds it ironic that this call came in while she was in the midst of reading the chapter about fear versus faith!

While preparing to go downstairs, she starts repeating the Scripture referenced by Tina earlier, *Do not be anxious about anything, but in every situation, by prayer and petition, with thanksgiving, present your requests to God* (Philippians 4:6 NIV). Then something she just read in chapter 4 enters her mind, "Are you operating in fear or faith? What motivates you in every situation? Spiritually, fear is a trick of the enemy, an entrapment to keep you from trusting in God. Fear is a snarl, a trap to cause you to take your eyes off God and stay focused on the problem."

Remember to breathe, remember to breathe, Laura says to herself. Then grabbing her purse and phone, she ensures the door is locked behind her before heading downstairs to the security office.

13

Laura enters the security office and is greeted by Officer Greg Maloney who introduces himself as the hotel security manager. He informs her that so far, there are no leads regarding her hotel room break-in. In fact, there were no matches from the fingerprint report.

He then directs her attention to three large screen monitors with video recordings, displaying pictures of people at different angle views. The video includes recordings from the day prior to Laura checking into the hotel on Tuesday. Laura is asked to view the footage up closely, but initially doesn't seem to recognize any familiar faces and becomes discouraged. When asked to take a closer look and take her time, she stares at them for several more minutes and is about to give up when faces of two people in a couple of the videos catch her attention.

Laura exclaims, "There, seated on that couch, almost hidden behind that large stone pillar, that person right there," pointing to a man who appeared to be in his mid-forties with a thick graying mustache. "That man who's wearing a Dodgers' cap and appearing to be hunched over a newspaper. And wait a minute, see that short lady who's standing about six feet from him, appearing to be talking on

THE GIRL FROM CHAPEL HILL

her cell phone? I vaguely remember seeing them together on my university campus about a month ago."

Laura frantically attempts to recall the university campus scene, puzzled about why these two people would be at this very resort during the same week she's here. Oh, yes, she's pretty sure she had caught a glimpse of them on her campus, but who were they? Who were they visiting? She's racking her brain, trying to remember more details. She was certain they were not regular staff members. Were they students? Wait, Laura remembers something and turns to Officer Maloney.

"These two were on campus chatting with one of my newest colleagues, Jessica Donaldson. I wasn't close enough to overhear their conversation. I was actually coming out of the library that is located in the building adjacent to where I work when I saw them at a distance. They appeared to be deeply involved in their conversation and scanning the area as they were chatting. I found it quite odd because as I recall, Jessica had mentioned that she was scheduled to teach a class during that exact time, and yet here she was, outside the building. Her back was to me, but I knew it was her from that funny-looking red wide-brimmed straw hat she was wearing. When I saw her in the parking lot earlier that morning, I remember thinking how strange it looked. Who wears a straw hat during the fall season?

"At any rate, you may find this interesting! Jessica is the one who highly recommended this resort hotel to me. I've only known her since last semester, but some way, she had managed to befriend me, and I am not usually that easily befriended. We've met over breakfast a couple of times.

During our first breakfast, we were talking about kids—of course, that's what moms do!. When she told me her son, James, goes to Smithdeal-Madison University, I chimed in by saying, 'That's amazing! My son is a sophomore at that university." According to Jessica, her son is a freshman. So having something in common, especially when it came to our kids, sort of ignited the flame. Even though we aren't that close, we enjoy comparing notes regarding them. Now thinking back, she was the one who started the conversation about parenting!

"Jessica is among the very shortlist of people who knew I would be coming here this week, but I hadn't shared how long I would be here. Perhaps it is just another coincidence. There have been plenty of 'it just so happened' things in my life lately."

Officer Maloney asks Laura for a description of her colleague, Jessica. After thinking for a minute, Laura provides the following description: "Caucasian, around forty-three years old, slightly taller than me [I'm five feet five]. She has short dark hair and wears glasses. Oh, she does have some freckles on her face, but they aren't that noticeable."

Laura's cell phone rings, and she hesitates to answer it, but when she looks at the caller ID, she answers it right away, her intuition telling her that it won't be welcoming news. She turns to Officer Maloney, and with her hand covering the mouthpiece, she gives him a pleading look, then asks that he give her a minute as this may be somehow related. He points to a nearby chair, off in a corner, and motions that she's free to use it. She motions for him to stay nearby.

"Hello, Laura, this is Anne. I hope you are enjoying your vacation. I am really sorry to bother you, but earlier today, I overheard a very peculiar conversation, and when your name was mentioned, I thought it was important enough to call you. I hope I am doing the right thing."

Laura's heart begins to pound faster, and she silently repeats, *Do not be anxious about anything, but in every situation, by prayer and petition, with thanksgiving, present your requests to God* (Philippians 4:6 NIV).

Pausing a moment to quiet her nerves, Laura thanks Anne for calling her right away, assuring her that she is indeed doing the right thing, then asks her to please continue.

"Laura, I was coming out of the staff lounge, and as I turned the corner, there was Jessica talking with this woman. Sounding very intense, they were discussing your whereabouts, and that you were planning to stay at the hotel for at least one week."

How would anyone know how long I was planning to stay? Laura is thinking.

"From where I was standing, I couldn't get a good glimpse of the other woman, and sorry to say, I did not recognize her voice. However, knowing how private you are and although the fact that they were discussing your whereabouts was odd enough, that wasn't what really got my attention. Now, Laura, I hope you know me well enough to know that I am not one to gossip or eavesdrops. Nope, but I got this weird feeling right away—call it a sixth sense or whatever—that something just wasn't quite right about their conversation, so there I was, stuck in my tracks around the corner from where they were standing. Jessica couldn't see me, but I got a quick peep at her, then I immediately backed up to hear what she was saying. Luckily, there was no one close by who would have called out my name. Otherwise, I would have been caught like a deer in a headlight. Yes, I would have been caught. The mere fact that I, a professor, was eavesdropping! Now, Laura, you know I pride myself on being a very detail-oriented professor. So I am really disappointed I can't give you a description of the lady who was with Jessica. I will tell you that her voice sounded like a Texan. Don't Texans have a certain drawl?"

Laura starts silently tapping her figures against the chair's arm, trying not to sound impatient as she waits for Anne to continue. Anne tends to beat around the bush and the barn and sometimes even the farm before getting back on track. So Laura sort of clears her throat as a gentle reminder for Anne to get closer to her point. It worked.

"I heard Jessica saying something like, 'Yes, our informants arrived at the hotel where Laura is staying a couple days ago and have been closely monitoring her. Nope, they mentioned that breaking into her room was only a distraction. It doesn't sound like it was enough.'"

"Wasn't enough for what?" Laura asks Anne, who quickly responds, "Now, now, Laura, I have no idea what this means. I was hoping you would know!"

Anne continues, "Their voices were going in and out. So I couldn't hear everything that was said. I did hear Jessica say something like, 'They said they have been instructed to step up their game because that's just not good enough.

They aren't sure why the repeated 'hang-up' phone calls didn't work. To my knowledge, Laura hasn't even reported the calls to the authorities yet. Nope, they don't want to go to that extreme, not just yet. Yes, yes, time is really running out, so again they will deploy more aggressive actions."

When Anne stopped talking, Laura tries to level her breathing, then asks if she had overheard anything else during Jessica's conversation.

"No, the two of them started walking away from me, rushing toward the cafeteria. I didn't think it would be a good idea to follow them. Besides, I couldn't keep up with them even if I wanted to with my aching feet and all." Anne chuckles.

Setting aside her thoughts about Anne's attempt at humor, especially during this time, Laura was baffled, frightened, and somewhat speechless. However, she did not want to let on to Anne that what she had just shared was horrible news; it was indeed very disturbing. She didn't know Anne well enough to trust her with any information. And she most definitely didn't want any gossip to spread throughout the campus.

"Well, that is really interesting, Anne. I can't imagine what this is all about, but I truly appreciate you calling me. It is probably some friends playing a prank. You know how that can be, especially around Halloween time. Even some grownups don't know how to behave! You know what I mean?" Laura tries to cover her nervousness with a little chuckle. "That even sounded like a fake chuckle to me," frowning, Laura says to herself, but then quickly adds, "Anne, would you please do me a favor? Don't share this information with anyone else. It may not mean anything, but it is a lot to think about."

To which Anne responded, "Now, now, Laura, I would never do such a thing. That would be gossiping, and as you must know, I'll be no party to that!"

"Okay, I've got to go now, but if you hear anything else, anything whatsoever, please don't hesitate to call me. I owe you big time. In fact, let's do lunch when I get back!"

After thanking her profusely, Laura hangs up the phone.

Now Officer Maloney had been standing nearby during the entire time, detecting from Laura's tone and facial expressions that the phone call was definitely unpleasant. Even though he could only hear what Laura was saying to the caller, it actually sounded like it was connected to what was happening to her at the hotel. He wished he could have recorded the telephone conversation. He lowers his head, not liking the sound of this at all!

Laura takes a deep breath while silently praying, *Do not be anxious about anything, but in every situation, by prayer and petition, with thanksgiving, present your requests to God* (Philippians 4:6 NIV). This has clearly become one of her favorite Scriptures as well. Then turning to Officer Maloney, she tries to repeat verbatim what she had just heard from Jessica as she watches him furiously take notes of this new information.

After listening to what Laura just shared, he asks if she has any idea who these people are and why they are seemingly trying to frighten her.

"Not really," she hesitantly replies, but she wonders if any of this has anything to do with her encounter with the stranger. She's really torn about whether to mention anything about the stranger's news, then opts against it.

However, he is very observant. Based on Laura's demeanor, particularly during her response, he suspects she is withholding some critical information. It is no accident that he decided to personally stay involved in Laura's case. He could have easily assigned it to one of his junior officers. However, based on the latest news from Laura, he's glad he followed his instinct. He not only has an excellent reputation as the hotel security manager, but as a retired police officer and investigator, he has a record of being one of the best in his field.

I'll need to gain her trust in order to help her, he surmises.

Officer Maloney asks Laura if she had contacted her local authorities regarding the repeated "hang-up" phone calls. She reluctantly admits that she had not made that a priority but plans to do so right now. So based on the recent information she received from Anne, while sitting in the privacy of the security office and with him urging her on, Laura finally makes that phone call to her local authorities. She wishes she had done so sooner.

Officer Maloney promises to investigate further in attempts to identify the man and woman who Laura had vaguely recognized in the video footage. Based on Laura's telephone conversation with Anne, if his suspicions are correct, these two people are the "informants" referenced by Jessica. That being the case, he needs to investigate their actions as soon as possible because Laura's life may be in danger!

After some quick thinking, Officer Maloney mentions that he has a friend who is a private investigator (PI), and that he may be able to do some research on Jessica's background (since this is out of his jurisdiction). He asks Laura if this is something she wants to pursue.

Laura, who had been wondering about Jessica's motives as well as her background, immediately agrees. "I thought I could trust her, but now I am just not sure about much of anything."

As a safety precaution, he asks Laura to check in with the security office at specific intervals during the day and just before she retires for the evening. He insists on escorting Laura back to her room over her objections. After unlocking her door, he steps inside her room to ensure it was safe for her to enter. He also double-checks her door locks to ensure they have not been tampered.

Finding nothing amiss, he turns to Laura and says, "If you think of anything else that you believe may be of importance, no matter how insignificant, please call me directly." He then leaves after handing her one of his business cards.

Finally, alone with her thoughts, Laura collapses onto her bed, breaks down and cries, totally dismayed at her current predicament.

Based on everything that has happened, it appears that someone is intent on making my life miserable, and that's putting it mildly. If what Anne overheard is true, there are some people somewhere out there in this world who may want to harm me and for what? Laura moans. Immediately, Laura's mind goes back to her encounter with the stranger, and she is convinced now more than ever that there is a connection between what Anne overheard and the stranger's news. "Heavenly Father, what should I do? Do I trust this information to Officer Maloney? Should I remain here for another few days, knowing that someone is watching me. Or should I return home not knowing what I'll find when I get there?"

Pray. Renew your mind. Pray. *Do not be anxious about anything, but in every situation, by prayer and petition, with thanksgiving, present your requests to God* (Philippians 4:6 NIV). That's what Laura hears in her spirit.

Dropping to her knees, she acknowledges that she is frightened and needs God's guidance and wisdom. She acknowledges that she is weak, but that God is strong. She thanks God for giving her clarity to move on, for strengthening her to withstand whatever is happening. She begins to quote Scriptures such as, *Trust in the Lord with all your heart. Lean not to your own understanding. In all your ways acknowledge Him and He shall direct your path* (Proverbs 3:5–6 KJV). She ends her prayer by saying, "Lord, I don't know what happens next. I don't know what to do, but I know You do, so my trust is in You. Amen."

14

Even though Laura doesn't realize it, God hears her cries, and help has already been sent to her. She just needs to trust God and follow the leading of His Holy Spirit.

Looking at her watch, Laura realizes it is 2:00 p.m., and she hadn't made her usual interval check-in with the security office. She also hasn't made contact with her son Mike yet. She's about to dial the security office when her cell phone rings. She answers it and hears a crackling sound, then a muffled voice.

After looking down at the caller ID, she is relieved to see her husband Drew's phone number. They hadn't spoken in over a week, even though she had left him several messages.

"Drew, how are you?"

No answer.

"Drew, where are you?"

No answer.

"Drew?"

Finally, she hears his voice, but it sounds very muffled. "Laura, what's going on? Why haven't you been picking up my calls? Where are you? Honey, I've called you several times and was wondering why I hadn't heard from you.

Laura, what's going on? Why haven't you been picking up my calls? Where are you?"

Laura can't understand why he keeps repeating the same words over and over.

"Drew, the last time I spoke with you I mentioned that we had been getting recurring 'hang-up' calls at the house."

"Laura, what's going on? Why haven't you been picking up my calls? Where are you?" More crackling sounds. "Laura, I haven't spoken with you about any recurring phone calls. What are you talking about?"

Oh no, thinks Laura, *something's not right.* "Drew, can you hear me? You keep repeating the same questions. Drew, are you back home or still overseas? We've got to talk. There's so much going on right now. Hello?" Then she hears a crackling sound after which the service is disconnected.

Silence. Dead silence.

When Laura attempts to call Drew's number, it goes straight into his voicemail. After several more attempts to reach him, she starts to worry.

Her cell phone rings again. She answers it right away, thinking it is Drew. However, there's breathing on the line, but no one is talking. After saying hello a few more times and receiving no response, she hangs up.

Her cell phone rings a third time, she picks it up but doesn't say hello. She knows it is not Drew's number, but the area code looks familiar.

"Who is calling?" she asks.

The caller identifies himself as John Franklin, dean of student affairs at Smithdeal-Madison University, Mike's college. Mr. Franklin is calling to check on Mike, stating that he hasn't been to class or been seen on campus in over a week and asks her if everything is okay. Alarmed, she asks if campus security is involved, which prompts Mr. Franklin to ask if there's any reason why they should be? With Jessica drama closing in on the forefront of her mind, Laura doesn't respond to his question, but lets him know she will follow up with him as soon as she hears from Mike and/or if she needs his assistance. After thanking him for alerting her, she hangs up, trying not to push the panic button.

"What was his name? Oh no, I can't recall his name." Shaken, Laura attempts to reach Mike again, but his phone goes straight to voicemail. She then contacts the twins, Marty and Matt, who have not spoken with their brother for a couple of days. Knowing the twins have full-time jobs, and with Mike's heavy class schedule, she isn't surprised they haven't spoken in two days. She mentions the call she received from the dean of Mike's college, and the twins promise to keep trying to reach their brother as well. Their attempts to reassure their mother that Mike is okay seemingly fall on deaf ears. So since they only live about an hour from Mike's campus, they promise to drop everything and drive to his college right away and stay in touch with her. They inform her that as soon as they hear or see Mike, they will notify her immediately. In the meantime, Laura keeps trying to reach both her husband and Mike. Two things really concern her: (1) it is not like Mike to ignore repeated calls from her, and (2) this is the first time she's received any news about him missing classes. Even though Mike is the youngest of her three sons, he's been the most responsible one when it comes to education; however, he's the least responsible one when it comes to his finances!

Laura is beside herself with worry. *Can this day get any worse?* she asks. First, the video footage of the two hotel strangers who are apparently stalking her; second, the telephone conversation with Anne; third, the weird call from her husband Drew that ended abruptly; fourth, the unidentified caller who insists on heavy breathing; and finally, not being able to reconnect with her husband or reach her youngest son all within a span of fifteen minutes.

Oh, and speaking of the weird call from Drew, what was it he had said about 'not having spoken with her regarding any hang-up phone calls?' What was that about? Didn't I talk with him on the phone about that? Am I losing my mind? moans Laura. Sensing a migraine headache creeping up on her, she downs a couple of pain pills.

There's no doubt in her mind, she needs help. She's so overcome with worry that she's having difficulty renewing her mind and getting any comfort from her favorite Scripture, *Do not be anxious about anything, but in every situation, by prayer and petition, with thanksgiving, present your requests to God* (Philippians 4:6 NIV).

Laura feels light-headed and realizes she hasn't eaten anything since breakfast. Pacing back and forth, she grabs an apple that was left over from the morning's breakfast. Without eating the apple, she calls Officer Maloney, but the call goes straight to his voicemail, and she leaves a message for him to call her right away.

Laura was saying to herself, *I've got to talk with someone. I feel like I am about to lose it. I know, I'll try to reach*

Tina! Laura dials her number to let her know that she may need to leave immediately to locate her son Mike. When her voicemail comes on, Laura leaves her a rushed message to return her call as soon as she can.

Oblivion. The last thing Laura remembers before being overtaken by darkness and fainting is the sound of a phone ringing.

15

After several unsuccessful attempts to reach Laura by phone, Officer Maloney arrives at her door, along with one of his female security officers. They repeatedly knock on her door while calling out her name—no answer. Finally, using their passkey, they enter and find an unconscious Laura lying facedown on the floor. They notice a small amount of blood on the right side of her face, near her hairline.

While Officer Maloney calls for emergency medical service (EMS), the security officer checks Laura's airway, breathing and circulation, turning her face upward. After about five minutes, she starts to come around. By the time the EMS personnel arrive, Laura is lying face up with her feet elevated. She's physically feeling better, although an emotional wreck. One EMS technician checks her vital signs, then the source of the bleeding. Apparently, she had hit the side of her face when she fell. The technician asks her a series of questions; she provides very vague responses to most of them. After a second check, they note her vital signs are fine, and that a preliminary cause of fainting is possibly attributed to anxiety and under eating. Rambling that she must leave right away to find her son Mike, Laura declines the offer to be escorted to the hospital. She promises to follow up with her primary care provider as soon as is practical. After much prompting by Officer Maloney, Laura finally eats the apple. Recalling the last thing she remembered doing before passing out, she checks the desk clock and realizes she must have been out for roughly twenty minutes.

Just as the EMS is leaving, Tina rushes through the door. She had listened to Laura's urgent voicemail message, and when she couldn't get her on the phone, she had wasted no time getting to her room.

Laura nervously stares first at Tina, then at Officer Maloney, trying to decide what she should do or say next. She is embarrassed at all of the attention she is receiving and tries to cover up her anxiety but fails miserably. He gestures to his security officer that it is okay for her to leave. Laura thanks him and Tina for coming to her aid, and then after realizing they probably don't know each other, she introduces them.

Noticing that Laura still looks fragile and based on the advice of the EMS, he turns to ask Tina if she will order dinner for Laura. Tina, who is keeping a very observant eye on Laura, was one step ahead of him. She was already on the phone calling in dinner orders. Since she had planned to stay a while with Laura, she ordered one for herself as well. She also cleared her calendar for the remainder of the evening.

Finally, as things begin to settle down, Laura turns to them both and apologizes for being a hot mess. She tells them about the series of phone calls she received within a span of fifteen minutes, the unidentified heavy breather (sounded like another one of those "hang-up" calls), a fragmented and confusing call from her husband, and finally, the dean of student affairs at Mike's college, informing her that he was missing. She also shared that she had contacted her twins about Mike being missing, and that they were on their way to his college. She mentioned that she was on standby for their call but was wrestling with driving there herself. She stated that if she didn't hear back from her twins very shortly, she would be taking to the road. Officer Maloney and Tina exchange glances, each mentally acknowledging that there was no way Laura was in any state of mind to be traveling alone.

Once again, he senses there is another piece of information that Laura is withholding but doesn't want to probe, especially with Tina standing nearby. Not knowing the extent of their relationship, he doesn't want to place either of them in an awkward position.

Laura's cell phone rings, and noticing it is Marty's number, she answers it right away. She's holding her breath, but when she hears all three sons on the other end, she is so relieved to find out that Mike is truly okay. Laura turns on the speakerphone so Officer Maloney and Tina can hear firsthand. After so many strange phone calls, she doesn't trust herself not to have a witness or two!

"Mom, I returned your call about thirty minutes ago and left you a voicemail message. I wasn't sure why you had called me several times. I was in class most of the day. But at any rate, I left you a message, letting you know that I was okay. That was before Marty and Matt got here, scaring the heck out of me!" Mike chuckles.

Thinking back, Laura recalls that after she had come around and saw people hovering over her, she had been so disoriented that she didn't think to check her voicemail right away. Had she done so, she would have found out that while she was passed out, Mike had indeed finally returned her call, leaving her a message that he was fine.

Hearing the voices of all three sons on the phone is sheer pleasure to Laura, especially in the midst of everything she is going through. Even though they are constantly talking over each other as they normally do, she picks up on what is most important.

Marty and Matt had just arrived at Mike's dorm room and, to their surprise, had found him playing video games. He was actually playing games when he should have been studying. They snitched as they teased their little brother! Those two weren't the only ones surprised. Mike was clearly stunned to see his big brothers at his college in the middle of the day and then to find out he was supposed to be missing. Apparently, his phone had been stolen while he was in the cafeteria. He remembered placing it on his food tray while he turned around to chat with someone, yet somehow it had strangely resurfaced on a hall table outside his dorm room. Mike had no idea why his mother or his brothers had called him so many times; he clearly didn't know that the dean had reported him missing. Regardless, he admitted how happy he was to see them!

On the telephone, talking with their mother, the twins sound like it was amusing that their youngest brother is the last to know that he has been missing in action. Mike informs them that he had been on campus all day and has kept to his usual routine. So why would the dean think he was missing? Simply mind-boggling. They are laughing and talking at the same time. All of this to the chagrin and, admittedly, relief of their mother.

None of them has any idea what turmoil their mother is enduring! Since her sons are still at Mike's college, Laura asks all three to go to the dean's office and try to find out what was going on and then to call her back immediately. She stresses to all three that this is a serious matter. About ten minutes later, she receives a call from Dean Franklin, who has her on speakerphone with all three of her sons present. He seems to be just as confused as they were; he states emphatically that he has not called her or reported Mike as missing. Dean Franklin voices some suspicion when Mike chimes in and informs him that his phone had been stolen and then resurfaced outside his dorm room. Without raising any undue alarm, he needs to determine if there is any connection to the stolen phone and someone reporting Mike as missing. So he immediately asks Laura's permission to hold onto the phone so he can have the security team dust it for fingerprints immediately. While Mike certainly doesn't want to be without his phone, he obliges. Dean Franklin promises to provide him with a loaner phone within the hour. Clearly concerned, whether this is some sort of terrible joke or not, he promises to do everything possible to get to the bottom of any shenanigan immediately. Needless to say, Dean Franklin does not find it amusing at all! Before hanging up, he apologizes profusely to Laura on behalf of the college.

While Officer Maloney and Tina are indeed thankful that Laura had allowed them to listen in on her phone conversations via the speakerphone, neither know what to make of the calls. However, based on the information Laura had received from Anne earlier, Officer Maloney is certain there is a connection. Having already solicited the help of his PI friend, he makes a note to pass this information on to him as well.

After approximately fifteen minutes, he informs Laura that he's about to leave but promises to be in touch as soon as he hears anything. Laura hasn't had an opportunity to update Tina on the latest happenings, so she is clearly confused. She promises to bring her up-to-date.

Frowning as he stares at Laura, apparently trying to read her mind, Officer Maloney starts to ask her something but then decides against it. Instead, he reminds her of their agreement that for her safety, she will check in periodically with the security office. As he turns to leave, Laura asks that he not leave yet because there is additional critical information she needs to share, and she'd like both of them to hear it.

Officer Maloney and Tina stare at each other. Then they look at Laura as she stumbles to her feet and starts wandering around the room. Trembling but resolved, she starts to share her frightening encounter with the stranger and the shocking news he delivered.

"A strange man approached me a little over a week ago with some shocking news about my family history. You see, there I was, coming out of the grocery store near my home, and this man called out to me. He didn't introduce himself, but there was something a little familiar about him. [I can't place whether I had seen him before, or whether he just reminded me of someone else.] At any rate to gain my attention, he quickly told me some news about my life that totally caught me off guard and left me almost devastated, questioning my very identity. The backlash from this news, combined with the numerous disturbing 'hang-up' phone calls, really got to me so much so that I needed to get away. This is the main reason I took a break from work and came to this resort." Laura is about to share exactly what the stranger told her when they are interrupted by a knock on the door. Dinner is being delivered. What timing!

While he believes the remainder of her story will be critical to her case, Officer Maloney is even more concerned with her overall well-being. So in light of her earlier fainting episode, he thinks it best if Laura eats her dinner before finishing her story. He can tell that whatever she plans to share with them is going to be a serious undertaking, and without eating, it will possibly take an even greater toll on her. So he tells them to eat dinner, and he will either return to her room, or they can meet him in his office in about an hour.

Tina seems to have a calming effect on Laura for whatever reason, and so perhaps some "girl time" will be good medicine before continuing our meeting, he is thinking.

They agree to meet him in his office in an hour.

Tina gives Laura a hug and tells her that whatever she is going through, everything will work out for her good. "Come on, let's eat and get your strength back!"

As she prepares to pray over their food, Laura smiles and thanks her again for coming.

16

During dinner, she attempts to get Laura's mind off her current situation by encouraging her to be strong, to trust God, and to believe that better days are ahead.

Tina says to Laura, "I am here to encourage you that you will have a safe landing if you trust in the Lord! Yes, I know, you may be thinking, 'Look at what's happening in my life right now. Everywhere I turn, I hear bad news.' However, Laura, God is your shelter from this storm in your life. There will be other storms, and the same God will still be there! For there is a safe landing. Just you wait and see.

"I can tell you from personal experience, even in the midst of any tragedies you may be experiencing, even in the midst of life's horrors, even in the midst of any disappointments you may have had, even in the midst of any heartaches and pains, with God's help, you can and you will survive!

"When you allow your mind to focus on the good news that there is a safe landing in Jesus Christ, you will be all right. When you give your burdens totally over to the Lord, you will have a safe landing. When you truly believe in His Word, you will have a safe landing.

"Check this scenario—have you ever been in an airplane when there was turbulence? The plane begins to shake, and fear tries to paralyze you. Things around you start to shake, people around you start to moan, complain, and doubt, then you hear the calming voice of the pilot, saying, 'We are just going through a rough spot, but this turbulence will be over soon.' Your mind starts to rest, things around you start to settle down, and you have the reassurance that things are going to be okay because the pilot has spoken. Then the plane descends, and you land safely on the ground. Well, God wants to be your pilot, the pilot of all pilots, and even when things around you become rocky, His Word assures you that it is going to be okay. His Word assures you that this is only a temporary situation, and you are going to land safely in His arms. Yes, there is shelter in His arms.

"All of us will experience some type of storm in our life at one point or another. Some of us may be tempted to go and hide from the storm. Others may wish it would go away, or they live in fear. However, we know that God has given us everything we need to ride it out. We have the power to choose what we will do in the midst of it. Yes, the storms of life will rage in our lives, and sometimes we may not know our left from our right, our head from our toe. Sometimes we may feel like we don't even know what day it is, but as Christians, we have everything we need to ride it out."

During the entire time Tina had been speaking, Laura seems to be clinging to her every word. It is like Tina is throwing her a lifeline, and she is intent on grabbing it and holding on as if her very life depends on it. Laura compares herself to a sponge, for she's trying so desperately to soak it all in.

When Tina pauses and asks if she was okay, Laura smiles and says she feels a whole lot better. Then she asks Tina to pray for her strength and faith.

"I need all the prayer I can get," Laura says to herself. She knows she is going through a really bad storm and needs to lean in on God as never before. She needs to hold on to Him as an anchor and let Him be her pilot so she can safely land with her mind intact. She remembers a Scripture she heard somewhere along the way that said something about "no weapon formed against you will prosper." She finds it interesting that it doesn't say, "It would not form," but "it would not prosper." She has no idea who is using a weapon to form against her, but she so wants to trust that God won't allow it to prosper in her life.

As usual, Tina is seeking God's wisdom on just what to pray on behalf of her new friend. She knows there was still much she doesn't know about Laura, but she is determined to trust in God Who knows everything about everyone. So taking a deep breath, she reaches over and takes Laura's hands and prays.

"Heavenly Father, we give You honor and praise because of Who You are. We are so grateful that we can come to You in our weakest hour and get strength. Father, Your Word says where two or three are coming together in Your Name, touching and agreeing, You are in the midst. So, Heavenly Father, we thank You for listening to our prayer, and we acknowledge we can't make it on our own without Your strength and guidance.

We thank You, God, for giving each of us a measure of faith that we can hold onto, especially during storms in our lives. So now, Father, I ask that You strengthen Laura right now as only You can. Heavenly Father, please help her renew her mind and cling to Your Word to strengthen her faith. Heavenly Father, help her to trust You more in spite of how things look. Heavenly Father, we thank You that no weapon formed against Laura will prosper. In the precious name of Jesus, we pray. Amen!"

Strengthened by their prayer, they finish dinner and hurry to the security office to meet with Officer Maloney.

17

Officer Maloney greets them warmly as they enter his office. Even though it is after 7:00 p.m., and he normally would have been off work, he has been waiting patiently for them. If the rest of her story supports what he already suspects, some investigation into her case will need to extend beyond the walls of the hotel. That being the case, he knows it will be outside the boundaries of his jurisdiction. Therefore, he needs to pass all information on to his PI friend, which is why he ask and obtain her permission to record what she is about to share. Not wanting to delay any further, he motions them to a table with chairs and prepares to listen to what he labels "the rest of her story."

Laura appears drained but insists she is determined to share the rest of her story with them as it's been a burden to bear alone. While she had not forgotten the stranger's instructions not to tell anyone what he had informed her, she decides to throw caution to the wind.

What's he going to do about it? thinks Laura as she takes a deep breath and begins to unload.

"As I mentioned earlier, there was this stranger who called out to me as I was coming out of the grocery store a little over one week ago. The man didn't really introduce himself. He was about four feet away from me when he first called out my name. I was wondering if he was someone I had met earlier. I hesitated because although he was wearing sunshades and a hat, there was something about him that was tugging at my memory. Later on, I remembered something that may be of importance—he had a slight limp that caused him to drag his left foot. And I was trying to recall where I had previously seen a man with that type of limp. At any rate, as he continued to walk toward me, he called out my name again, but this time, he used my full name, Laura Marie Parker-Harris, and that really got my attention because I don't use a hyphenated last name. I literally stopped in my tracks.

"From my peripheral view, I could see people around us were beginning to stare first at him, then at me. He noticed it too, but it didn't seem to matter. He looked determined to get my full attention so he could get on with his business at hand.

"Then there we were face-to-face, well, actually I had to look up to him because he was so tall. He immediately began to tell me some facts about my own life. Some things were so personal that I could no longer ignore this stranger or think that our 'meeting' was just a random encounter. Among other things, he told me I was reared from birth by my grandmother Grace Parker who had died fifteen years ago. That was a fact. He told me that my maiden name was the same as my mother's maiden name, not my father's. That was a fact. I recall occasionally questioning Mama about my father and my last name. She would always smile and dismiss my questions by saying, 'You are a Parker. Always be proud of that name.'

"This stranger told me that my birth mother had been widowed for several years now. That was a fact. And finally, this stranger told me that I had received a four-year anonymous grant to attend Williams & McIntire University. He knew that this grant was based on conditions that it be renewed yearly, provided I continued to meet the academic criteria. That was a fact.

"At this point, I was too stunned to even say anything. As if knowing so much about my life wasn't enough to totally mess with my head, this stranger, this man who knew so much about me, yet I knew absolutely nothing about him, proceeded to tell me a bit of shocking news that caused me to question my very identity. He was very careful about how much information he shared. But he did tell me that my father, who I never knew, was not dead but was very much alive.

"Now you see, based on limited information I picked up during my childhood, whether it was gossip or not, my mother never heard from my father after she became pregnant with me. Then around my preteen years, I had heard that she had received news my father had died. She was always so *hush-hush* about my father. So whether she ever attempted to verify this information remains a mystery to me. By this time, she had already married, relocated to New York and had three other children.

"Nevertheless, this stranger told me that he had been hired by someone, and he didn't say by who, to arrange a meeting between my father and me. He also told me that he had specific instructions to contact me first without any warning [hence, the purpose of our meeting in front of the grocery store]. He also said that he was instructed to follow up with me later to schedule this meeting at a specific time and place to be identified later. He ended the brief encounter by saying that it was very important to keep this information private. But that he would be in touch with me later with further details and directions.

"And here I am, trying to figure out why another stranger who calls himself my father—if what this stranger is saying is true—would wait all this time to reach out to me. Where does this story end? Is this story part of a bigger story? Is there any connection between this and everything else that has been happening to me lately? I mean, just look at everything that has happened over the past month or so. Why the unrelenting hang-up phone calls? Why was my room the only one that was broken into during the fire alarm? Why is someone apparently stalking me, or am I just being paranoid? What about the mysterious phone call with my husband? Why did someone call me about my son being missing? Was his phone stolen a part of any conspiracy? Was Anne telling me the truth? If so, does Jessica have anything to do with any of this? Are these merely coincidences? What if someone actually wants to kill me? Am I being paranoid? Did I ask that already?

"Sometimes I think I am losing my mind, instead of renewing it."

Resting her head on the table, Laura begins to moan, feeling the beginning of another one of those migraine headaches. "I am not sure I can take much more of this!

How much longer until this stranger contacts me? And where is my husband?"

He stops the recording and turns to Laura. "Regarding your hotel room break-in and the two people in our video footage, we have investigators on it and will definitely get back with you very soon. I will contact my PI friend and get this recorded information to him right away. Have you heard anything back from the local authorities regarding the 'hang-up' phone calls to your home?"

"Nothing yet, but I will contact them again when I get home. I've definitely decided to leave tomorrow. I guess it really doesn't matter where I am. The ghosts still find a way to haunt me," replies Laura.

Looking at Laura, Tina symbolically gestures to her with "praying hands," a motion that is not lost on Officer Maloney. Interesting, he smiles at Tina as he asks himself, *What is it about her that makes me want to get to know her better?*

Lifting her head from the table, she moans again about taking something for her headache, and Tina, taking the cue, stands up to leave. They both head to the door, saying good night to him. When he asks if either of them needs an escort, they respond no. Instead, they hold up their cell phones to each other, signaling they will talk with each other until Laura is safely in her room. Then they leave for the elevator.

Laura arrives safely to her room and hangs up the phone with Tina, agreeing to call her if she needs anything. She's so focused on taking some pain meds to relieve her relentless headache that she doesn't notice the envelope that had been slid underneath her door. After taking some pain meds, Laura debates whether to take a couple of sleeping pills also. Then yielding to an inner voice that gently says, "Cast your cares on Me for I am with you always," she resists the urge for sleeping pills and relaxes until her headache resides.

It is just a little after 10:00 p.m., and although she's weary, sleep is slow to come because her thoughts keep turning to the day's sequence of events. In an effort to ease her tension, she does a little reading before going to bed. Flipping through the pages of Dr. Anderson's book, she finds chapter 5 ("Resting during Turbulent Times") to be so appropriate for how she is currently feeling. Propping herself up on a pillow, she starts reading.

"*Be still, and know that I am God. I will be exalted among the heathen. I will be exalted in the earth* [Psalm 46:10 KJV]. This Scripture is always a calming reminder of what rest truly means, and it tells us to calm ourselves, to put aside all those distractions, and to simply trust God for who He is!

"Each of you will experience some turbulent times in our life at one point or another. God never promised you a rose garden…or so the song goes. But He did promise to always be with you. He told you to trust Him.

"Even in the quiet times, when it doesn't seem like He's listening, you should cease from worrying. Just be still and rest in Him, for He is God. Look at what the Bible says about this, *Then you will call upon Me and go and pray to Me, and I will listen to you. And you will seek Me and find Me, when you search for Me with all your heart* [Jeremiah

29:12–13 KJV]. Something marvelous happens in the still-ness of the night. There's a calm. There's a peace that sur-passes all understanding.

"Just say to yourself, 'Lord, I don't understand why I am going through this turbulent time, but because You are my banner, I am going to rest in You. Lord, I don't understand why I received this bad report, but because You are my banner, my Jehovah Nissi, I am going to trust You. Lord, I don't understand why my paycheck is not lining up with my bills, but because You are Jehovah Jirah, my Provider, I am going to trust You. Lord, I just don't know, but because You are all these things to me and so much more, I am going to rest in You during turbulent times. Lord, I just don't know which way to turn, but I do know that You are all these things to me. I am going to focus on the good and perfect gifts that come from above and lean not to my own understanding.'

"You see, when you decide to rest during turbulent times, you simply are demonstrating that you know who God is, and you know that He's got your back. With grace and mercy following you all of your days, you know you will be okay.

"If you ignore the distractions, focus on His promises, you can rest. That's what having faith in God is all about. You need to rest during turbulent times so that you can hear from God. Search for Him with all your heart sincerely.

"How many of you know that your greatest weapon during turbulent times / storm days is praising God? Oh yes, you need to praise God in spite of the problem, in spite of the challenges, in spite of the obstacles, and in spite of what is or is not. You need to praise God regardless of what you may be going through even right now. Yes, you can have joy while you are in the midst of turbulent times.

"Oh sure, you are walking around men, appearing full of life, but deep down, you feel there is something still missing. Instead of praising God, you are focusing on the problem. In your dark places, in your monumental experiences, in your valley, do you truly believe that this same God can and will bring restoration to your soul? You need to rest and trust Him at all times.

"I believe that oftentimes, if not all the time, you may go through turbulent times because God is allowing these circumstances to come about to make you and mold you, to conform to His image. Oftentimes you cry out, 'Satan, get behind me,' or 'Satan, you are defeated,' when Satan may not have anything to do with your turbulent times. And so, he's laughing at you and glad to be taking the credit for what is happening in your life when he knows he had nothing to do with that circumstance. Oftentimes you give Satan too much credit!

"These turbulent/dry bone experiences will prove useful to you when you are in a position to lift up someone else. So when you are in the valley, just give praises to God. Yes, thank Him in spite of the problems. Why? Because that's what the Word tells us to do.

"Is there anything too hard for God? Are your shoulders stronger than God's? Take your burdens to Him and leave them there. Remember that He is a rewarder of those who diligently seek Him. God desires for His people to be free of bondage, of shackles. That's why it is so important to praise Him at all times. For He truly inhabits the praises of His people! Remember, just to reiterate—it is through your praises that your breakthroughs will come. The Bible tells us that heaven and earth may pass away, but God's Word will never fail.

"Well, you say, this all sounds good. I really wish I had that kind of faith. I really wish I could step out in this knowledge. Have we forgotten that it only takes a mustard-seed kind of faith to step out and trust God? Just praise Him!

"You can ride out the storm during turbulent times, for the sun will come out tomorrow. Whatever you may be going through at this very moment, just know it is only temporary. It may seem like the storm will last forever, but it won't. Jesus says it will be okay. Just put your trust in the Master, for He knows the plans He has for you. He is the Master Planner!

"Yes, sometimes the storm gets very dark and gloomy. It is like a tunnel. But there is light at the end of the tunnel. Just trust in Him! You may be sad or heavy burdened, but the Bible says, *He healeth the broken in heart, and bindeth up their wounds* [Psalm 147:3 KJV]. Rest in His Word."

Calm. Peaceful. Tranquil. Serene. Reading such inspirational words is so much better than sleeping pills! That's the last thing she remembers thinking before drifting off to sleep, forgetting to set her alarm or check her phone.

18

Upon awakening, Laura is amazed just how rested she feels. She stares down at Dr. Anderson's book that she had been reading before she fell asleep last night. Looking at the title of chapter 5 ("Resting during Turbulent Times"), she can't help smiling. God knew exactly what type of sleeping pill she needed!

Around 9:00 a.m., as she's getting dressed to drive home, Laura finally notices the envelope that had been slid under her door. Since the envelope isn't hotel stationary, she doesn't suspect it is a list of hotel charges. Quickly opening it, she sees the simple typed note in ALL CAPS and red lettering that read "I KNOW WHERE YOUR HUSBAND WAS LAST NIGHT, DO YOU?"

"My husband? Who is the world would leave such a note? Is my husband cheating on me? Is he still overseas? Why hasn't he called me back? Is this real?" she asks herself. Should she call the police? Should she call Tina or Officer Maloney? She looks at the clock and frantically ponders what she should do, wondering if this is merely another hoax designed to mess with her head.

Laura's pacing around the room, almost at the point of hysteria. She starts to call Tina, then remembers she's facilitating a session this morning. She calls Officer Maloney on his cell number, no answer. She then calls the security office and is informed by the receptionist that he is temporarily on a leave of absence. The receptionist then politely asks Laura if there is someone else who may be able to assist her. Too stunned to answer, Laura hangs up the phone. She doesn't know what "temporarily on a leave of absence" implies.

Wait, didn't I just see him last night? Wouldn't he have informed me if he was going to be out of the office, considering everything that is happening to me? I don't know what to make of this! Laura cries out loud.

Just as she's feeling a little woozy and anxious that another migraine may be coming on, her cell phone rings. It is the local authorities regarding the recurring "hang-up" phone calls to her home. They were able to trace the calls to an overseas number; however, that number has recently been disconnected. They failed in their attempts to locate the last owner of that number, apparently a fake identity was used. When she asked if they knew the date of the last call from that number to her house, they confirmed it was Tuesday, which was the day she had left for the resort. Laura finds that interesting and mentally makes a note to pass this information on to Officer Maloney if she is able to make contact with him again. Absolutely confounded, Laura vaguely remembers thanking them as she hangs up the phone.

When a phone rings again, Laura is surprised to see it is the hotel room phone as she hasn't gotten any calls on that number. Ignoring the nagging migraine headache that is trying to rise to the surface, bringing all of its ugliness with it, she hesitantly picks up the phone, and to her relief, it is Officer Maloney's voice! She wants to ask him right away about his job situation but gets the feeling he's rushing and being guarded. When he hints that he prefers not to talk over the phone for obvious reasons, she gets the picture but then becomes even more worried. Laura rushes to tell him about the note that was left under her door. He tells her to hold on to it so he can have it dusted for fingerprints. He then tells her that the two of them need to meet at a different location right away. She has lots of questions but remains silent.

He asks Laura if she remembers the female security officer who accompanied him to her room yesterday? When Laura responded that she did, he continued.

"Okay, for your safety, I've asked her to come up to your room and escort you downstairs to the front of the hotel, where I'll be waiting. Can you be ready in ten minutes?"

Laura responds that she can.

"There, the two of us will walk over to the Westchester Hotel together. It is a long story, Laura, but I really need you to trust me. One more thing, remember to peep through the keyhole to make sure it is the security officer before you unlock the door," he instructs her.

Laura thanks him nervously and ends the call. Then grabbing her purse, she paces back and forth until she hears the knock on her door.

She peeps through the keyhole, and even though she recognizes the female security officer, she asks to see her credentials before removing the chain lock.

After initial greetings, Laura says to the officer, "I am sorry that I may seem a bit overly paranoid at this point with all that has happened to me lately."

After the officer replies that she fully understands, there is an uncomfortable silence as she escorts Laura outside of the hotel. Both of them are relieved to see Officer Maloney standing nearby. He thanks his security officer and tries to reassure her by saying in a very low voice, "We will get to the bottom of whatever is going on with my job situation. Don't you worry. In the meantime, I need you to be my eyes and ears."

The two of them have worked together for many years at two different companies. He trusted her; she trusted him. He knew he needed to lean heavily on this trust now as never before.

With a frenzied look, Laura turns to say something to him, but he motions her to keep quiet until they arrive inside the Westchester Hotel, which is only about a couple of blocks away. Once there, he is met by one of his comrades, who is on the security team there. His comrade escorts the two of them to a private room. At which time, he leaves them alone so they can talk freely. There's a table set up with breakfast Danishes, fruit and some coffee and tea. At the sight of the food, Laura realizes she hasn't eaten anything all morning and, with tears in her eyes, thanks him for his thoughtfulness.

As he can imagine, Laura has so many unanswered questions. After he makes sure she's comfortable, insisting that she eats something, he starts talking.

"I know Tina is facilitating a seminar at this hotel, so I took the liberty of leaving her a message to meet us in this office when she gets a break."

Reading Laura's mind, he continues, "Yes, we exchanged contact information, and since I can tell how close the two of you seem to be, I figured you might need to see a friendlier face other than mine of course." He half chuckles as he grabs a cup of coffee. "Laura, let me start by trying to ease your mind regarding my employment status as I am sure that is weighing heavily on your mind. After you and Tina left my office last night, my boss called and informed me that I was being placed on an administrative leave of absence for an alleged severe misconduct. Based on our working relationship, he knew I had been set up. Apparently, one of the guests claimed I made unwanted sexual advances toward her. I had never even met this lady and can assure you without a doubt that I did no such thing. I am not only appalled but upset that someone is obviously making this serious allegation to steer me away from your case. But don't you fret. I have been in tougher spots before based on my line of work. And yes, I am confident now more than ever that this false claim is linked to what's going on with your situation.

"Even though my reputation is, well, let me say 'impeccable,' protocol dictates that I be placed on administrative leave pending the outcome of an investigation. As I'm sure you could tell, my security officer was pretty upset as are most of my team members. It's a wonderful feeling to work with a team who trusts you no matter what may happen. Yes, this is a serious disruption or distraction, however one may view it. However, I am confident that I will be cleared of any wrongdoings very soon. Shortly after I was relieved of my duties based on this allegation, this guest somehow disappeared, leaving no trace. I figure she was probably paid by someone to make this false claim. If the hotel manager doesn't hear back from her in forty-eight hours, they will consider this matter closed. Until that happens, I am not allowed on the premises of the Regal Bay Resort Hotel.

"I am privileged to be given some office space here at the Westchester. I have several old acquaintances who work here. In the meantime, I am working very closely with my PI friend. Based on the information compiled so far, we are getting very close.

"Okay, here's what I know. Regarding those two guests that you recognized on the hotel's video footage, our investigation determined that they registered at the hotel using fake identity. They checked out as soon as we started making inquiries. The identification they used was reported stolen by someone in Texas about one month ago. Regarding the credit cards used by the two guests, we have contacted the companies. We are waiting for feedback to determine if there's a possibility that the two guests—or should I call them—thieves—are known by the actual credit card holders. We realize this is a long shot, but the investigators are doing everything they can to solve this case.

"We believe these two thieves were also responsible for setting off the alarm to cause a frenzy while your room was invaded. Our internal investigation also revealed that someone had sneaked into the restaurant's kitchen. They attempted to mix some type of dangerous substance into a tea canister. I learned from the staff that you ordered tea with some of your meals. I hate to believe this poisonous tea could have made its way to your room! Apparently when the night cleaning staff returned to finish up some last-minute tasks, they heard a noise and saw the back of someone running out of the kitchen's side door. We believe the door had been intentionally left unlocked. Yes, we are looking into all of this as some of our security measures clearly need to be tightened.

"Among other things, since there was no evidence of the door to your room being tampered with or lock being broken, we are left to conclude there is a mole on the hotel staff. Obviously, that's most unfortunate. We are aggressively checking into this now and plan to expose whoever the employee is very soon.

"Now this is what my PI friend's investigation uncovered regarding your colleague, Jessica. According to our research, there is no Jessica Donaldson on staff at Chestnut-Patterson University. Further research revealed, there is no Jessica Donaldson anywhere who fits the description you provided. And if I recall correctly, you mentioned that this Jessica told you she has a son that attends the same school as your son Mike. Well, according to our research, yes, you guessed it. There is no James Donaldson at Smithdeal-Madison University, nor is there any Jessica Donaldson with a son named James. So it would appear that a fake Jessica befriended you to gain your trust and some of your personal information. I would bet that if you contacted your colleague, Anne, who by the way, is a legitimate, albeit nosey individual, you will find that this Jessica has totally 'left the building.'

"Last, thanks for giving Dean Franklin your permission to speak with my PI friend. Per Dean Franklin, the school's security team dusted Mike's phone for fingerprints, and as you probably already guessed, it was clean. Naturally, that leads us to conclude that his phone was stolen for the explicit purpose of using it to prevent any calls between you and your son. We suspected that, especially when an imposter, who claimed to be the dean of Mike's school, called you regarding him being missing. To think that this scheme also included someone at Mike's school tells us that this well-thought-out plan involved multiple persons.

"Laura, all of this combined with the numerous 'hang-up' phone calls and now this mysterious note that was left under your door lead us to believe that someone is trying to drive you crazy. For what purpose? We certainly can't answer that, but perhaps you can?"

Noting that Laura either can't answer that or chooses not to, he continues. "It sounds like there's more to this story, but that's our opinion based on the information we have to date. I am concerned that someone may increase efforts to do this or, worse yet, put your life in some type of physical danger." Looking at Laura's face, he grimaces and apologizes for making her even more uncomfortable.

"Oh, before I forget, may I have that note? I wanted to personally take a look at it before passing it on to the hotel security team as soon as possible. That's why I didn't ask you to give it directly to my security officer."

Laura grabs her purse, then she pulls out the envelope to retrieve the note that is inside of it. Shockingly, she sees only a blank piece of paper. There is no ink on the paper! The typed message has totally disappeared! She looks inside the envelope again. She looks inside her purse again. She then haphazardly proceeds to dump all of its contents onto the table, some spilling over onto the floor. No typed note. Nothing!

He stares questionably at Laura, who by now is beside herself with bewilderment as she almost yells at him, "I promise you, there was a large typed note in red lettering. It was right here in this envelope that I placed in my purse just before leaving the hotel room. That typed note clearly said something like 'I KNOW WHERE YOUR HUSBAND WAS LAST NIGHT, DO YOU?' I came straight here from my hotel room. So I know I never had a chance to leave it unattended."

Laura searches through her contents again. Nothing! She looks at him and pleads, "Please tell me you believe me. Please tell me you know I am not making this stuff up. I understand you don't know me that well. So I'm pretty sure what I am sharing with you may sound way off base. But please believe me, I am not crazy! I am a very rational person. Please tell me you believe me! Look, if you can't tell me that, then please tell me this is all a dream, a terrible dream, and I am about to wake up at any minute now!"

Around 11:00 a.m., as Tina knocks on the door and comes into the office, she finds the two of them standing there, looking dumbfounded at each other, and shaking their heads! Laura is perspiring like crazy and looking bewildered like she just saw a ghost! Officer Maloney is looking like what he just witnessed is so unreal that he's totally at a loss for words. Judging by the look on his face, she can tell that Laura's story, whatever it has evolved into, has definitely thrown him for a loop! She has absolutely no idea what just transpired within the last hour but is confident of one thing. It's definitely not good news for Laura!

Seeing Tina standing there is a welcoming sight for him as he is at a loss for how to respond to Laura. Thinking quickly, he seizes the moment as a great opportunity to excuse himself and slip out of the room. He does this for two reasons. First, he needs to get some air and regain his composure as he ponders what to say or do next. Second, he wants to allow the two ladies some time alone. Based on his observation of how they previously interacted with each other, he hopes Tina can use some of her magic to bring some calmness into the room. He will defer to Laura on just how much of this latest news to share with her friend.

Unbelievable! Can this story get any worse? he says to himself and softly closes the door behind him.

19

Quickly taking in the scene before her, she does not wait for Laura to explain anything. She simply rushes over and hugs her. Then she bends down to pick up the personal items that are scattered on the floor, placing them upon the table. Tina then silently begins to pray ever so softly as she waits for guidance from the Holy Spirit. Then leading Laura to a chair, she pours her a glass of water from the nearby pitcher, and when she sees the food on the table, most of which hasn't been touched, she asks, "Have you eaten anything?"

When Laura responds that she has, Tina hesitates because it clearly doesn't appear Laura has eaten much, but she doesn't want to sound like she's "mothering" her. So rather than continue down that road, she simply asks, "Do you want to pray right now?"

Laura, still looking confounded, stares up at her and asks, "Where is God in all of this?"

Tina's mind goes back in time when she had cried out that very same question. She was having a particularly tough time and was waiting on God to answer a prayer. Thinking back to that season in her life, she looks at Laura and shares her story.

"Let me start by sharing my story about when I was in a very dry season. I was waiting for God to move on a particular situation in my life. I was watching and waiting. It seemed He was quiet. It seemed as if God hadn't even heard my cry. I called out to Him many, many times. I felt so alone.

"Where are You, Lord? Can't You see me way down here, just struggling with all of the cares of this world? Where are You, Lord? I can't even hear You whispering my name. Where are You, Lord? Please come quickly and dry my weeping eyes. It's too quiet. I don't feel anything. I don't see anything. I don't hear anything. But You told me to trust You. You told me not to lean on my own under-standing. You told me that You would never, ever leave me. Where are You, Lord? It seems I'm left here all by myself, all forsaken, and I just can't bear the thought of it all.

"While I was waiting for my miracle, was I embracing the stillness? No. While I was waiting for an answer to my prayer, was I remembering what He had already done for me? Was I thanking Him in advance for what I was expect-ing Him to do? No, I was not. While I was waiting for a break through, had I armed myself with spiritual weap-ons? Was I continuously praising Him and giving Him the Glory for who He is? No, I was not. Here's something I didn't understand then, but I understand now. To avoid a hostage takeover, especially in the stillness, it was import-ant to arm myself with spiritual weapons.

"Remember what Dr. Anderson said about this? During times of difficulties, one of the greatest weapons is praising God, just start praising and thanking God for who He is and for what He has already done. I'm talking about a praise party where you shut out everything else and focus on Him! There is one thing for certain, praising God will definitely take your mind off the current situation. There's no way you can praise Him and worry at the same time. When your prayers seem to have gone unanswered, praise God and cast your worries on Him. This is how you embrace the stillness."

Tina looks at Laura to see if she's lost her attention, and so far, she appears to be hanging in there.

"Laura, I haven't forgotten your question," she says, still praying inwardly for guidance. Although Tina recognizes this may not be the best time to start quoting all sorts of Scriptures, she knows that she needs to rely on the best source she has, and without a doubt, that's the Word of God. Based on her own experience, she understands why Laura feels the need to question if God is still with her. However, she is also fully aware that Laura's battle is spiritual and not physical. Even though she doesn't quote it to Laura, there's this one Scripture that immediately comes to the forefront of her mind, *For we wrestle not against flesh and blood, but against principalities, against powers, against the rulers of the darkness of this world, against spiritual wickedness in high places* (Ephesians 6:12 KJV).

So gazing at her friend, she believes God will be pleased with her response.

"Remember this, God has not left you. This is the time when you must draw on the reservoir of strength like you have never, ever done before. Laura, just like you need physical food to survive, now more than ever, you will also need to rely on spiritual food to get through this storm. I know you may not want to hear this right now, and yes, I may sound like a broken record, but drawing upon these Scriptures will give you the strength you so desperately need. Laura, my friend, this is the time when you will need to *trust in the Lord with all your heart and lean not to your own understanding.* This is the moment when you need to remember, *In all of your ways, you will need to acknowledge God and allow Him to direct your path* [Proverbs 3:5–6]. Always remember what God tells us in His Word, 'No weapon formed against you is going to prosper.' I get it. It might feel as if you are at the end of the rope, but I want to remind you that you are not, so be strong in the Lord and tie a knot and hold on. Sounds familiar?

"You asked where is God in all of this? The answer is 'God, the Great I AM, is right where He always is in the beginning, in the middle, and in the end of it all. Remember, we are talking about God Who was in the beginning and Who created the end—way before any of us were born. God is and always will be your very present help in these troubling times. God is the One who is keeping your mind. It may not seem like it, it may not feel like it, but God is still in control. He doesn't tell us to trust our feelings, for our feelings will lead us down a dangerous road. He tells us to trust in Him, for He cares for us.

"So whatever is going on in your life right now, although it may seem insurmountable, there is nothing too hard for God. Get this—and I know this may sound crazy, and yes, I can imagine what your response may be to what I am about to say next because there have been times in my life when I have had the same questions you have right now. Nevertheless, I'm going to say it anyway, so don't throw anything at me. Here it is—the Bible tells us, *And we know that all things work together for good to them that love God, to them who are the called according to his purpose* [Romans 8:28 KJV].

"Yes, I know, right? But since you didn't throw anything at me yet, I'll keep talking. As Dr. Anderson would say, 'Don't allow the circumstances, regardless of what they are, to dictate how you are going to use your faith.' The Bible says, *Now faith is confidence in what we hope for and assurance about what we do not see* [Hebrew 11:1 NIV]. So stand on the many promises of God, stand still and know that God is still God, even in the midst of such mess!"

Laura is amazed how she is able to absorb much of what Tina is saying. It was merely a few minutes ago when she was about to toss in the towel! She is being strengthened through her words of encouragement. She looks around the room, starts placing her personal contents back inside her purse, then finally turns to Tina, and wholeheartedly says, "Thank you for reminding me that no weapon formed against me is going to prosper. This trusting thing is really new to me. I'm trying to do the best I can with what I know!"

Then smiling as she musters up all the energy she can, Laura takes Tina's outstretched hands and joins her in prayer.

After their prayer, Laura updates her on the latest developments. Tina is trying extremely hard to hold back her own tears. She smiles and simply says, "My dear friend, I believe your story. YOU ARE NOT LOSING YOUR MIND!"

They chat for a while. Then Tina senses a "release" in her spirit and knows that Laura will be okay. Yes, the road ahead may be rough, and yes, she will still have more storms to endure. But the clouds will pass over soon, and the sun will break through. She knows that God will give Laura the fortitude to press on toward a wonderful, expected, and bright future. She plans to keep on praying that God gives Laura wisdom and protection.

Before she leaves her friend, Tina grasps her hands and tells her, "Remember faith that has not been tested cannot be trusted. You cannot have a testimony unless you have a test. And, wow, what a testimony you will have! Our God will supply your every need and will allow you to triumph over this tribulation. Yes, you will come out of it stronger than ever. And get this, God will empower you to use your testimony to help others! Just walk by faith and not by sight. Trust in God!"

Looking upward and thanking God inwardly, Tina leaves the office, returning to the conference room where she is scheduled to meet with Dr. Anderson before her next seminar. She passes Officer Maloney in the hallway and gives him a "thumbs up" and the most beautiful smile he has ever seen.

Officer Maloney reenters the office and is surprised to see such a remarkable change in Laura's countenance.

Chuckling, he says to himself, *Tina has struck again!* He remains very curious about the common thread in these two ladies' relationship. He's wondering, "What is it about this lady that gives Laura the strength to endure during such craziness in her life? After all of this is over, I definitely plan to have a talk with her!" Little does he know that it is not Tina but God Who makes the difference.

Laura conveys her plans to him just as she had informed Tina earlier. She definitely plans to leave for home as soon as she is packed. Neither of them believes she should be driving alone at this time. However, she has made up her mind and promises to stay in touch, checking in with one of them periodically while she's on the road. She also promises to let them know once she arrives home. Seeing that her mind is already made up, Office Maloney encourages her to hang in there, and that, as he has already promised, he will be in touch with her soon.

Before he escorts Laura back to her hotel, he makes sure she puts his personal cell number in her phone. He makes a mental note to ask her later to get a new phone as he's not sure if hers is secure. Then after arriving back at the Regal Bay Resort Hotel, he calls the security office to provide an escort to her room. She thanks him profusely, but he responds by saying, "I'm only doing my job. Please take extra care of yourself and, again, stay in touch."

When they arrive at her hotel room, having been told in advance that Laura plans to check out shortly, the security officer keeps watch outside of her door as Laura completes her packing. Then the officer escorts her to the lobby. As she prepares to check out at the reception desk around 1:00 p.m., she glances around at all the people who are circulating in the lobby. She doesn't see any familiar faces or anything that looks out of the ordinary. So she takes a deep breath and leaves the hotel. She is determined not to allow paranoia to overshadow the peace she is embracing.

Heading toward the parking lot, she finds herself repeating, "Thank You, God, for not giving me the spirit of fear but of love and of power and of a sound mind." Everything is calm. Even though she doesn't understand it all, she has such a peace and is thanking God for never leaving her alone.

A phrase pops in her head, *He never said the mountains would be removed right away, but He promises to give me the strength to climb them. He never said the storms would pass right away, but He gives me whatever I need to sustain the mighty winds!*

"Wow!" she says out loud.

She arrives safely to her car and checks her surroundings but doesn't see anything amiss.

Thank God! she says to herself as she gets in, buckles up, and starts to drive out of the parking lot. Thinking about the stranger and when she might hear from him again, the girl from Chapel Hill is reminded that she has more hurdles to jump. But for now, she will just take it one moment at a time.

20

As she drives away from the resort area and takes one more glance through the rearview mirror, Laura becomes so filled with mixed emotions; tears of joy threaten to blur her vision. Thinking back over the past few days, there's been a lot of good and bad happenings. However, for now, she chooses to focus on the good things. She is thankful that God allowed her to strengthen her faith. She is thankful that God allowed her to reconnect with Him in a more personal, meaningful way. She has never experienced such a connection. She thanks Him for the wonderful gift of forgiveness. She thanks Him for freeing her from past guilt. Freedom never felt so good. She thanks Him for sending an angel her way in the form of her new friend, Tina. She also thanks Him for Officer Maloney. Even though he had said that he had only done his job, she believed he had gone over and beyond to help her, especially with soliciting the aid of his PI friend.

She thinks about Mama's faith and is in awe as she thanks God for helping her to develop her own faith. She knows she can't rely on her beloved Mama's faith as she did when she was that little girl in Chapel Hill. She now understands faith is a very personal thing. She knows, even though she doesn't always use it, the measure of faith that God gave to her is still there, very much alive. Although the past few days have been both a blessing and a terror, she admits that God's hands have certainly been at work right there with her as she held on to the end of her rope.

She's thinking back to when she first arrived at the hotel. Never in a hundred years would she have imagined all the things that had transpired to her in such a few short days.

"Yes, I came here to get away from stuff, but somehow that stuff just followed me."

But she is thankful that the same God Who has been with her during this past week is the same God who will be with her regardless of what happens in the future. She is so thankful that God enabled her to leave the resort with her mind still intact. Considering everything she endured, except for her reconnection with God, she believes "having her mind still intact" is the best blessing of them all!

After driving for about thirty minutes, Laura stares over at the passenger's seat where she had placed Dr. Anderson's book, *The Battles Within, Enough Is Enough.*

She smiles and says, "I came to this resort for rest and relaxation, and although I found neither of those things here, I'm leaving armed with so much more!" But wait, she continues talking to herself, "I may not have found rest or relaxation for the body, but I did find rest for my soul!" Then she recalls one of the Scriptures she had heard and repeated it several times, "*I can do all things through Christ Who gives me strength.*"

Then she remembers something that Dr. Anderson said at the beginning of her seminar, "Know this—when you yield to this wonderful gift of His precious Holy Spirit, you will be able to boldly make a wholehearted, sincere determination that regardless of the circumstances, you will not be subjected to the battles within! These battles will succumb to the will of the Master!"

Come what may, Laura could hardly wait to be able to tell the rest of her story.

Looking down at her fuel gauge, Laura realizes she will need to stop for gas soon. So she starts searching for the next gas station exit. About fifteen minutes later, as she's about to exit, her phone rings, and it is Officer Maloney.

"Hello, Laura, sorry, no time to explain right now, but tell me your exact location," he says.

She tells him as much as she knows, including the exit number and adds, "I'm about to pull over to a gas station. Is something wrong?" She's trying hard not to sound frantic.

Without answering her, he says, "Don't panic. We have everything under control. I just need you to do exactly as I say. Got it?" Not waiting for her response, he continues. "I need you to get to that gas station as fast as you can. One of my security officers is in touch with our local police who will contact a police officer in the jurisdiction where you are, and they will meet you at the gas station. Listen carefully, whatever you do, don't turn off your ignition! Don't drive up to any gas pumps. Once you get to the station, drive to an open area and exit your car as quickly as you can. You should see officers arrive very soon. Stay on the phone with me the entire time. The officers in that area have been given the make and model of your vehicle."

Her palms start sweating, and she barely keeps the car on the road, but Laura is determined not to panic as she approaches the gas station. She lets him know she has arrived there. Again, he instructs her not to turn off the car ignition but to get out of the car quickly. She gets out of the car, determined to hold onto her phone. She leaves her car engine running.

He keeps talking with her on the phone. He gives the impression he doesn't want to reveal too much while she is waiting for the police officers to arrive. With her adrenalin high, she knows this is pretty serious, about as serious as it gets for him to be rambling off all these instructions!

Within five minutes, she sees two police vehicles arriving, and shortly afterward, she sees three officers approaching her cautiously, showing their identification. Backing away from her car, she looks toward the police officers and, for the first time, notices the police canine near her car.

Laura is silently praying while halfway stumbling away from her car. Everything starts to happen so quickly, but in her mind, it's in slow motion. As one officer swiftly takes her to an even safer distance from her car, another officer motions to the canine, who starts sniffing around the car, and the third officer serves as a backup.

Officer Maloney finally lets her know what is happening.

"Laura, literally a few minutes ago, we were able to identify the mole, the hotel employee who had been aiding and abetting the imposters. During an extensive interview process, the employee panicked and started talking. Apparently, someone placed a car bomb with a seventy-five-minute timer underneath your vehicle. If our information is correct, it has been set to go off at precisely seventy-five minutes from the time you started driving away from the hotel or as soon as you turn off the ignition. Laura, can you hear me? Laura?"

At this point, Laura drops her phone and faints. An officer, who is now within arm's length, catches her before she hits the ground. He then carries her to one of the police vehicles. Another officer picks up her phone that had fallen to the ground and starts talking with Officer Maloney. He assures him that they have the situation under control; that Laura has passed out and is now lying in the back seat of a police vehicle. Officer Maloney is beside himself with worry.

By this time, the police officers are attempting to maintain order with the crowd of bystanders who are assembling, pointing, and panicking. Finally, the canine locates the device. The bomb squad safely disarms it and removes it from Laura's car. Laura's personal belongings are removed from her car and placed into the police vehicle. Her car is taken to the nearest police station and impounded for further investigation. All this happens while Laura remains in a semiconscious state. Meanwhile, paramedics arrive on the scene and escort Laura to a nearby hospital.

Officer Maloney has remained on the phone the entire time, responding to the numerous questions raised by the police officers. They give him the name of the hospital where Laura is being taken. He hangs up to call Tina immediately.

21

Unbeknownst to her, a female police officer stands guard outside of her hospital room. Laura continues to go in and out of consciousness, solely due to anxiety and exhaustion. Her dreams are filled with images of car bombs, Drew, the stranger, memories of Mama, Western television shows, the haunting phone calls, and typed notes with words that keep evaporating. A few times, the hospital staff overhears her as she cries out for Mama. While these dream images come and go, there's one vision that remains constant—Tina kneeling beside her bedside, continually praying for her.

In the meantime, Officer Maloney's PI friend has finally made contact with Laura's husband, Drew. He had arrived back in the states and was on his way home when he got the phone call about Laura's hospitalization. According to Drew, he had missed several connecting flights due to some scheduling mix-ups. For whatever reasons, his office couldn't provide any rationale about the mix-ups. While he was overseas, his cell phone had periodically malfunctioned. After getting a new phone, which took longer than expected since he was overseas, he had made several attempts to contact Laura. However, for whatever reason, the calls always appeared to be misdirected. When he couldn't reach her, he had called all three sons, leaving several messages. By the time he was informed of the planned car bomb incident by the PI, his nerves were raw. He had so many unanswered questions. He also appeared to be extremely concerned about Laura and anxious to get to her right away.

Yes, the two of us will certainly have a lot of catching up to do, Drew is thinking.

When Laura finally comes around, she turns to say something to Tina, but she's not in the room. Shaking her head, she asks the nearby medical attendant about her car and her cell phone but is strongly encouraged to get as much rest as she can and not to worry about anything. She is also informed that a police officer will want to ask her some questions later.

As if being alone in a strange hospital isn't unnerving enough, the hospital insists on keeping her overnight for observations. Laura's not happy about this, but she is too weak to put up a fight. She does remembers asking someone if her husband had been contacted, to which there was no response. However, somewhere from deep within her, she remembers hearing these words over and over again, *Do not be anxious about anything, but in every situation, by prayer and petition, with thanksgiving, present your requests to God* (Philippians 4:6 NIV).

Morning finally comes. Laura believes she is still dreaming. Gradually opening her eyes, adjusting to the room's lights as she comes out of much-needed sleep, she's trying to get a grip on her surroundings. Her mind is still fuzzy, and she's not used to the different sounds, seemingly coming from all over the place, wherever she is. The brain fog slowly clears, and she remembers she is in a hospital. But before the harsh reality of what landed her there sets in, something wonderful and least expected happens. She smells a very familiar cologne, opens her eyes wider, looks up, and finds herself staring into the eyes of her husband.

"Drew, is that really you?" she whispers.

Her husband, looking very exhausted and tired, is staring down at her with such warmth and concern that her whispers turn into cries. She's calling out his name over and over again. She tries to cast aside any negative thoughts regarding the possibility that he may have been involved in any schemes to harm her. She simply refuses to accept that notion.

As he leans down to pull her up to him and she reaches up to touch his bearded face to make sure she's not still dreaming, she can't stop the tears from falling.

"I'm so sorry," he says.

"I'm sorry too," she replies.

They both are overjoyed to see each other. No other words are necessary. She silently thanks God for safely bringing her husband back home. Yes, even though they are in a hospital, she knows home is wherever they are together. Between sobs, hugs, and kisses, sounding incoherent, she tries to tell him what has been happening, but all he wants to know right now is if she's okay.

As he helps her sit up in the bed and props the pillow behind her, asking if she's comfortable, he keeps saying, "Lala, everything will be okay." Calling her by his nickname for her, he continues, "Lala, we'll get through all of this stuff together as long as you are okay. Nothing else matters as long as you tell me you are okay."

In her eyes, he's the most beautiful sight she has seen in quite some time! Still very drowsy, she's resisting the temptation to fall asleep again for fear he may suddenly disappear! Even though Drew notices how fragile she looks, he tries to look upbeat. He rings for the nurse, who comes in and checks Laura's vital signs. She makes a note that her blood pressure is still slightly elevated.

Outside in the hallway, the police officer hears their voices, and after getting permission from the nurse, she enters Laura's hospital room. The officer begins to ask some questions that might help their investigation into the attempted car bombing. Officer Maloney had provided much of the information. The officer is attempting to fill in the missing pieces. Laura looks over at Drew and, after taking a deep breath, proceeds to answer as many questions as she feels comfortable doing. Glancing over at him again, she asks him not to leave the room, and she nervously smiles. She can see that Drew is puzzled. She promises to update him as soon as they get out of there. It's not clear how much information has been shared with him. But for now, she just wants to get this interview over with and go home.

After the officer leaves the room, the nurse returns and checks her vital signs again. She promises to touch base with the doctor to see how soon Laura can go home. Meanwhile, around 9:30 a.m., her breakfast tray arrives, and Laura forces herself to eat a little, sharing most of it with Drew.

After consulting with the on-call doctor, the nurse returns and gives Laura the green light to leave. She is instructed to follow up with her primary care provider as soon as possible.

"Where have I previously heard that?" Laura asks herself, then remembers and says, "Yes, I remember now. Wow, what a week!"

Shortly afterward, her cell phone is returned. She notices several missed calls, including two from Marty and Mike, one from Tina, and one from an unrecognized number. Since Drew had informed her that he had spoken with their sons earlier, she decides to wait until she's home to call them. When Laura sees Tina's phone number, she looks over at Drew, who has never left her side.

"Would you please ask my friend Tina to return to the room?" she asks.

Laura assumes that she is somewhere nearby, perhaps in the hallway. He looks puzzled and says he hasn't met anyone named Tina but will check with the nursing station. Wondering if she is hallucinating, he leaves out of the room. He returns with a nurse who informs them that there's no one on their team whose name is Tina. The nurse also checks with the police officer who has been on watch outside of her room all night. With the exception of the medical staff and her husband, no one has entered her room. Laura notices that Drew and the nurse exchange puzzled looks, but neither says anything further about this "Tina" person.

While waiting to be discharged from the hospital, the nurse's station transfers a call to her from Officer Maloney.

After learning that she is feeling better, he strongly advises her not to use her cell phone but to get a replacement with a different phone number. Their investigation uncovered that her cell phone is indeed tapped. She promises to do so right away.

She is glad to hear from him. She is especially relieved to learn that he has been cleared of any alleged wrongdoings and is officially back on the job. Smiling to herself, she tells him, "You never were off the job, for you were always there, helping me." Before hanging up, she asks him to check in on Tina periodically. To which he laughs and responds, "Glad to have gotten your approval." She has an inkling that his life is about to change significantly but in a good way!

After she hangs up with him, she tells Drew about her cell phone being tapped. He tells her not to worry, that he will contact the telephone service provider as soon as they get home. For now, they both agree to use his phone only.

Another call is put through from the nurse's station. This time, it's Tina. She informs Laura that she had just spoken with Officer Maloney, and he recommended that she call the nurse's station rather than her cell phone. Somewhat confused, Laura asks if she had come to visit her in the hospital. When Tina responds that she had not, at first, Laura is stunned but quickly recovers. Stealing a glance at Drew who is nearby, she whispers to her that she can hardly wait to tell her about a vision she had while in and out of consciousness, a vision of her praying and interceding on her behalf. They chat for a minute longer and promise to keep in touch. She does her best to reassure her friend that she is okay and healthy enough to leave the hospital.

Before hanging up, she tells Tina, "Oh, by the way, his first name is Greg," and they hear each other laughing as they end the call.

Since the car bomb investigation is ongoing, the police will need to retain her car. That's not a problem since she will be going home in Drew's rental car. The police officer had delivered her suitcase and other personal items to her hospital room. So after gathering her belongings, they finally leave the hospital around 1:00 p.m.

22

They are about two hours away from home, which gives Drew plenty of time to think. Except for the brief stop he makes at a convenience store to grab sandwiches for the road, the drive home is quiet and uneventful. Occasionally he glances over at Laura, who appears to be sleeping so peacefully. He has so many unanswered questions, but he's more concerned about her health than anything else. He doesn't want to cause her any additional stress by bringing up unpleasant topics. Additionally, the doctor has advised that she rest as much as possible. Drew's mind keeps going over snippets of information he picked up during his initial phone conversation with the PI. He's also thinking about the line of questions raised by the police officer who interviewed Laura in the hospital.

There's another matter that's puzzling him. He asked her if she wanted him to call her job and let them know she would be on leave for at least a week or so due to illness. He was taken back to learn that she had already informed them of her need to take off for about three months.

Why hadn't she bothered to tell me something as serious as this? thinks Drew. It wasn't about the income because his salary was sufficient to comfortably sustain them for at least three months. However, major decisions, especially where finances were involved, were meant to be jointly made. This was something they had agreed upon several years back when they had first married.

Perhaps she did leave me a message regarding this. After all, my phone has been acting weird. I don't want to make any wrong assumptions, Drew says to himself.

Shortly after he arrived by her hospital bedside, he had overheard her talking in her sleep about meeting some stranger. What stranger? Also, after talking with their sons earlier this morning, he had learned that someone had posed as the dean at Mike's school and reported him missing to Laura. Why? And the most terrifying of all the news he had received was the fact that someone had apparently placed a bomb underneath her car! For what reason would someone want to kill her? What other secret was she keeping from him? Drew felt like he was about to come out of his skin with these and so many other mind-boggling questions.

To top it all off, during his initial phone conversation with the PI, he couldn't shake the feeling that he was being interrogated as if he was a suspect in an investigation. That clearly didn't set well with him. And during that conversation, he also sensed that he was not getting the entire story.

Why not? What in the world is happening? Drew keeps asking himself.

Yes, so many questions, he's thinking. But he was willing to wait for an explanation.

After he gets Laura settled comfortably at home and she feels up to it, he figures they will have plenty of catching up to do. Looking over at her again, he starts thinking about their strained relationship. This has been on his mind for quite some time. He knew the amount of time he spent traveling was taking its toll on their marriage. However, he detected there was much more to it than that. Both of them had always had demanding jobs but had managed to weather the relationship storms. However, during this season of the year, their relationship was especially strained, yet he could not get Laura to open up about what was bothering her.

"Is it me?" Drew often finds himself asking.

Whenever he was home, Laura would sometimes have sleeping fits or at least that's what he called them. These episodes would sometimes cause her to scream out in the middle of the night. Occasionally, he would hear her softly weeping in the mornings after such sleeping fits. Whenever he would ask her about them, she would just shrug it off and say, "Just a bad dream."

Almost home, Laura stirs and wakes up, yawning. Turning to him, she says, "Honey, I have missed you so much. Why didn't you return my calls? There's a lot we need to discuss. Not just about things that happened over the past few days, but others things as well."

"Lala, I'm not sure what's going on or how to respond to your question because I never received any calls from you that I did not return. I was also wondering why you never returned my calls." Drew shakes his head. "This is very peculiar. Perhaps our calls didn't go through because I was having problems with my phone. I ended up getting a new one, but that took a while. Yes, I know we need to talk. I have a lot of questions, but we will have plenty of time to chat as soon as you feel better. For now, I just want you to rest."

Laura thinks that sounded like a reasonable explanation, except for the fragmented phone call when she has reminded him about the ongoing disturbing "hang-up" calls. His voice is muffled, and it sounds like he doesn't even know what she is referencing.

Drew continues, "By the way, I don't plan to go into the office and or do any traveling anytime soon, at least not until you are feeling much better. I'm also staying home with you until we are confident the police have apprehended the car bombing suspect and resolved this case." Looking over at Laura and noticing her concern, Drew adds, "No need to worry. I've already left a message with my office. Besides, with the latest technology, I will be able to work on some of the software development projects from home. Don't you think it's about time?" Smiling at her, he continues, "So you see, I can juggle my projects and be home to get on your nerves—both at the same time!

"Also, on Monday, we should get you scheduled for your follow-up appointment with your doctor."

Laura is touched by his apparent concern and wants to believe, to truly believe that it's genuine. She couldn't bear to find out that his attitude was just a charade.

If I ever need to trust him, this will definitely be the time, she says to herself.

"We are almost home. Is there anything you need from the store before we get to the house?" Drew asks.

Laura is tempted to have him stop at the pharmacy so she can get some more sleeping pills, just in case she needs them later. However, she resists the urge. "No, nothing from the store. However, I'll need to call the telephone service provider as soon as possible regarding my phone replacement."

Reading his mind, she quickly smiles, then adds, "Yes, I remember, you will take care of that for me."

Thinking about the boys, Laura continues, "Guess you know I feel so lost without my phone, and I have several people I need to call." Of course, she remembers that Drew had called the boys from the hospital, and they had agreed to hold off on telling them anything about the attempted car bomb incident. "Now I just want to get home as soon as possible. It seems like I've been gone for weeks, yet it's only been a few days," Laura responds.

It's 3:30 p.m., and they are finally home. Drew notices that Laura is still wobbly and pale-looking, so he insists she goes straight to bed while he fixes her something to eat. He can tell she has lost weight, but he decides against saying anything about it during this time.

Rummaging through the refrigerator and pantry, he fixes her a sandwich and heats up some canned soup. At the last minute, he remembers how much she enjoys her favorite tea and brews it.

I'll have to order out for dinner since I'm not much of a cook. He chuckles to himself as he takes the food upstairs to their bedroom.

Drew later calls their telephone service provider and arranges for a new cell phone and number to be delivered by express mail. He then goes outside to check the mail-box. Seeing that it contains mostly junk letters and circu-lars, he places them on the kitchen countertop and is about to sort through them when Laura calls down to him. He leaves the stack without going through it, which is why he doesn't notice the strange-looking red envelope addressed to Laura. The envelope has no return address or stamp and has a handwritten note that says "TO BE OPENED ASAP."

23

Upstairs in their bedroom, Drew is thankful that Laura has eaten at least half of her sandwich and drank her tea. She's sitting on the side of the bed with an opened Bible on her lap. He stares at her, then looks down at the Bible. Even though that's a strange scene, he doesn't say anything.

"Drew, I know you have lots of questions, and while I don't have all of the answers, I'd like to tell you what I do know." Half smiling to herself, she continues, "Before leaving for the resort, I had a different outlook on life. You see, while I was there, I had an unexpected opportunity to attend an amazing seminar at a conference that was held at another hotel in the area. I clearly had no intention of attending any type of seminar when I left here last Tuesday morning. I took this unplanned getaway because I was feeling overwhelmed by so much stuff. I thought getting away from the norm and spending some time resting and relaxing would be good for me."

Even though Drew is still puzzled why she never informed him about her need to get away due to stress, he doesn't say anything, and Laura continues, "Well, while that may have been my reason for going to the resort, it certainly didn't turn out that way. My plan was certainly not God's plan, for He had something much bigger in store for me. No, no, I'm not talking about the horrible things that happened this week. For I know God didn't cause those things, and we are still trying to figure out the responsible party or parties. But you see, even in the midst of a lot of unexplainable turmoil—and yes, they almost made me think I was losing my mind… I'll tell you about those later—something wonderful came out of it.

"For quite a while, I knew my life was missing something that even you couldn't fulfill. Yes, I admit I'm not always that open when it comes to expressing my feelings or what's on my mind. I promise you, with God's help, that will change.

"I met this wonderful person at the seminar, and with her help, I was able to reconnect with God in a way I thought would never happen. By the way, that person is my new friend, Tina.

"Honey, there's no doubt I believe that she and this seminar were like a gift from God. At any rate, I made a personal commitment to spend more time getting to know Him through prayer and Bible study. There are so many Scriptures that help with renewing my mind. I know, I know, but my mind clearly needs a new attitude.

"Renewing my mind, wow, I can't wait to tell you about that seminar discussion. Honey, I wanted to rush home and dust off my Bible. It's been on the shelf for way too long! There is so much more about this week that I want to tell you. But that will have to wait until later.

"For now, here's the real reason I need to talk with you right away. I need to tell you something that happened to me a very long time ago. It's been a secret that has weighed so heavily on me, and I believe it has something to do with me not trusting people so easily." Laura had thought about telling Drew that she had shared this secret with Tina but knew doing so probably wouldn't set well with him. She knew he would be hurt because she hadn't told him about it first.

"Drew, please don't look at me like that, I am not losing my mind!"

At this point, Drew is becoming extremely nervous but tries to maintain his composure.

In his mind, it sounds like she is rambling and going off course, but he was determined not to come across as being insensitive or disinterested. So for now, he was going to play along and see if he could make any sense or connection out of anything she was saying. As much as he wanted to ask her questions about her newfound passion for the Bible and about this imaginary friend Tina, he was intuitive enough to know that this was just a prelude to whatever it was she was building up her nerves to say. After twenty-four years of marriage, Drew was still learning how to be patient with his Lala. So he waits and waits, thinking to himself, *How long?*

After what seems like several minutes, she continues, "Honey, I know we've had some communication breakdowns, and a lot of that has been my fault." Drew, seeing Laura's pained look as she struggles for words, tries to interrupt her, but she's not having that. "Wait, don't say anything, please let me finish. I really need to get this out. Yes, yes, I'm fine. I've waited far too long already. I don't want to keep shutting you out. Drew, I love you, and I really need you to believe that. No more secrets, okay?"

Drew is trying so very hard to stay quiet while, at the same time, masking his expressions of fear and anxiety, for at this point, he becomes really afraid of whatever secret Laura is about to share with him.

Seeing how desperate she is to say whatever is on her mind, he finally says, "Okay, Lala, if you believe this is the right time, and you feel up to it, if you believe it's important enough stuff and shouldn't be put off any longer, I will trust your judgment. I love you, and I promise I will try my best to be quiet and listen carefully to whatever you feel you need to share." Then he sits in the lounge chair across from their bed and waits.

Laura's saying to herself, *Do not be anxious about anything, but in every situation, by prayer and petition, with thanksgiving, present your requests to God* (Philippians 4:6 NIV).

Even though she doesn't realize it at this exact moment, miles away in her hotel room, her new friend Tina gets a strong urge to pray for them. So she stops what she is doing and starts praying and interceding on their behalf.

Laura takes a deep breath, smiles, and says, "Okay, this is going to be difficult for me, but here goes. Let me start from the beginning—and trust me, that's a very long time ago."

Laura proceeds to tell Drew about her most horrible kept secret that awful Friday night in late autumn when she was nineteen years old and a freshman in college. Without going into details, she tells him that she was raped by a guy she had just met at a party, she tells him that she became pregnant by that same guy, and finally, she tells him about the worst regrettable decision of her life, her abortion.

Not looking at Drew, Laura's mind goes back to a few nights ago when she shared all of this with Tina. She couldn't believe she had so readily opened herself up to Tina. She recalls how she felt at that time. She was astonished that she had actually told her, who she scarcely knew, about that horrible part of her life. She's recalling the prayers and the many Scriptures that Tina had quoted. She's thinking about how she finally found the strength to forgive that boy. She's thinking about how she finally received and accepted God's forgiveness, something she so desperately had needed. She's thinking about the freedom that she now feels because of being forgiven and being able to forgive. She's thinking about her Heavenly Father and how His unconditional love for her has always been there, even when she didn't know it.

Sitting here with her head lowered (not in shame but in awe) and staring at the Bible that is still resting on her lap, it dawns on Laura that she has no more tears to shed for her beautiful baby girl. She is silently thanking God for giving her the strength to finally tell Drew. She's thinking about how her little girl is finally at rest. She's thinking about how peaceful this moment feels. She's thinking about how, even waiting for Drew's reaction, he doesn't push that peace away. Simply amazing! She marvels at just how awesome God is and how He transformed her heart. She marvels how He is more than able to change any situation with a wave of His hands!

Drew is stunned and speechless. He's trying to decide whether to wait for her to continue, for he gets the feeling that she has more to share or whether to pull her into his arms and hold her close. Such mixed emotions. Should he be angry that she withheld this secret from him even though it was years before they met? Or should he thank her for finally getting up enough nerve to tell him? Looking at her, he realizes without a shadow of a doubt, it's not a difficult choice to make, not difficult at all. When Laura finally looks up and into Drew's eyes, he sees something there he has not seen before. It's a good thing. Serene!

"Drew, can you ever forgive me for keeping this from you?" Although she has forgiven herself, for some reason, she yearns for her husband's forgiveness, for she knows she has allowed this secret to come between them.

Still raw with so many emotions and wanting to be extremely careful how he responds, he does what comes most natural to him when it relates to his dear Lala. He rushes over to her and hugs her as if he never, ever plans to let her go. He is crying for her; he wants so desperately to take her pain. He is crying for all the lost years when she carried this pain alone, and although he can't understand it, he is mourning for the baby that was part of his Lala.

Drew knows he will need to deal with the anger, bitterness, and resentment he feels toward that college boy with no name, that boy who took his Lala's innocence, that boy who would remain faceless to him. But for now, for a split second or maybe two, Drew has a natural strong urge to reach out and hit something, anything that would substitute for this faceless enemy. But with Lala's renewed relationship with God and their love for each other, some-how he knows, someway he believes she will have enough strength for both of them, and ultimately it will help him overcome his very raw emotions. For he knows to move forward, he will need to forgive that nameless, faceless boy.

They stare at each other for a long time and then, without saying anything else about the secret that stood between them all these years, they tighten their grip on each other as they smother each other with kisses. There's so much love between them there should never be any room for unforgiveness.

But because he knows she needs to hear him say it, he whispers in her ears while still holding her, "My Lala, do you know how much I love you. I loved you then, I love you now, and I always will for eternity. And of course, without a doubt, I forgive you with all my heart!"

Shifting her position to become eye level with him, Laura groggily murmurs that she has some recent news to share. She has made up her mind to talk about the infamous stranger. Obviously, Drew is anxious to hear what Laura has to say, particularly if it pertains to the investigation. However, gazing at her, he can tell she is struggling to stay alert. So he knows it is best to heed the hospital doctor's advice. Drew gently removes himself from their embrace, stands up, and pleads with her to get some sleep.

"Lala, I promise, I'm not going anywhere, and we will have plenty of time to talk after you've rested some more."

Laura hesitates, then without saying another word, she gives in. The last thing she remembers saying to herself before drifting off to sleep is, *I've got to tell him about the stranger's news before he finds out from someone else.* Then she turns over in their bed, pulls the covers tightly around her, and allows her body to give in to such wonderful, peaceful, blissful, sleep.

Before Drew turns to go downstairs to order dinner, he picks up Laura's Bible that had fallen from her lap onto the floor and places it on the nightstand. Looking at it again, he figures that after the investigation is over, he can chat with her about some things that had been on his mind recently. He finds it interesting that while Laura was reconnecting with God over the past few days, he had been pondering about how to approach her on seeking some marriage counseling.

Maybe we are both headed in the same direction. He smiles to himself as he leaves the bedroom.

24

After Drew orders dinner, he makes several phone calls, including one to the police officer who has been assigned to Laura's case. The police officer is working very closely with Officer Maloney and his PI friend. The officer informs Drew that other than being able to track the bomb device to a factory in Texas, there have been no new developments.

As Drew is sorting through the mail, he comes across the strange looking envelope addressed to Laura. The envelope has a typed note that says "open ASAP." It appears that someone simply dropped the envelope in their mailbox since it has no return address or stamp markings. Nervously, he turns the envelope over and over in his hand. He can't imagine what's in it. Just when he is trying to decide whether to go upstairs and wake Laura, the doorbell rings.

Their dinner has arrived. After he tips the driver, Drew prepares to take the food upstairs to Laura. His mind returns to the strange-looking envelope. Should he take it to Laura, along with her dinner, or should he wait for a more appropriate time? Drew believes if he gives the envelope to her tonight, it more than likely will cause additional stress.

Maybe I'm being overly protective. I hope I'm making the right decision, for I don't plan to give this envelope to her tonight, he says to himself. Rather he places it in a plastic bag just in case the authorities need it for evidence. Tomorrow, together they can decide whether to open it or hand it over to the authorities. For tonight, he tries to put it out of his mind and instead enjoys a peaceful dinner and a movie in their bedroom, something they have not done in quite some time.

Halfway through dinner, Drew shakes his head when he turns to say something to Laura about the movie and finds she has fallen asleep.

The next morning, when Laura wakes up and looks around, she doesn't see Drew anywhere in the bedroom. Then with a sigh of relief, she hears him downstairs in the kitchen, apparently trying to find something to fix for breakfast. She laughs to herself, thinking about Drew and his chef abilities. As she's preparing to go downstairs to put him out of his misery, she starts to think about the movie she had attempted to watch last night. Her mind had actually been on her encounter with the stranger and her all-consuming need to tell Drew about it as soon as she could.

Out of the blue, she remembers something! Stopping in her tracks, she gets this sharp memory of her college graduation!

I remember, yes, I remember where I saw that stranger or at least someone who walked with a similar type limp.

She rushes downstairs to the kitchen, determined to tell her story to Drew.

When she finds him staring inside their refrigerator, she smiles to herself and says, "Good morning, honey, I'm okay to take over the chef duties, but for now, can we just have some toast and juice? We have got to talk!"

Drew smiles, looking happy to be relieved of his chef duties. Then just as quickly, he thinks about the doctor's advice and is still concerned that she may be overexerting herself. However, he sees her determination as she takes over. She pops some bread into the toaster and pours a cup of coffee for him and a glass of juice for herself. Drew reluctantly sits down at the table and waits expectedly.

"If you just hear me out, I promise you a full breakfast right afterward, okay?" Seeing his nod, she says, "Here goes…As I was coming out of the grocery store a little less than two weeks ago, I met this stranger who approached me with some rather shocking news."

Hearing Laura mention the word *stranger* jogs his memory, and he thinks about the strange letter that he has put aside last night. As Laura sits down to eat her toast, Drew abruptly gets up to retrieve the strange-looking envelope from inside the plastic bag. This interruption catches Laura off guard, and she's about to annoyingly ask him to "please pay attention" when she sees what he's holding up in his hands, a strange-looking envelope! She is stunned and starts trembling. Drew sees her reaction, especially with the expression of dread on her face. He is glad he didn't give it to her last night. Yet he remains concerned about what it all might imply. He asks Laura if they need to hand it over to the authorities.

Laura continues to gawk at the envelope, then says to Drew, "I've got a feeling this envelope contains information related to my encounter to the stranger. I've been trying to tell you about this man I met!"

Drew hands her the envelope. She is holding it so tightly in her hand as if she's afraid it will somehow disappear. She struggles to shake off the memory of the previous incident when a note was left under her hotel room door and how the typed letters magically evaporated into thin air. She hasn't mentioned this to Drew yet and is not sure if he will ever believe that bizarre story. She still has difficulty believing it herself!

After regaining her composure, she tells Drew that she feels the need to continue her story, crazy or not, before opening the envelope. "After all, at least we know there's no ticking time bomb inside the envelope!" she adds.

Drew sees no humor in her comments, but before he has an opportunity to respond, she rushes on.

"Honey, I never knew my father and was always led to believe that my mother hadn't heard anything from him after she became pregnant with me. When I was a preteen, I vaguely recall hearing that someone had sent a message to my mother that he had died. The first time I saw my birth certificate was at the age of sixteen when I applied for my driver's license. Not surprisingly, the space for my father's name was left blank.

"As you know, not too long after we met, I shared all of this with you. But here's the shocking news. This stranger, who seemed to know a lot about my life, told me that my father was alive and wants to meet with me! The stranger told me that he would get back with me to schedule a meeting.

"I believe this envelope right here is about the pending meeting. I'm not sure how I feel about meeting a father I thought was deceased, especially after all of these years. I just find this whole situation so bizarre. I have so many unanswered questions. Why now? I'm forty-seven years old. So why, after all these years, is he reaching out to me?"

Nervously, she hands the envelope back to Drew and asks that he open it and read the contents to her. So with her watching very closely, he opens the envelope, stares at her, and begins to read.

"This is PI Fletcher. Sorry I didn't give you my name when we met earlier. I was asked to withhold that information. I was hired by someone who is close to your father. For personal reasons, this person is asking to see you before you meet with him. Meeting is arranged for Monday at noon at the following downtown location. The McIntire Building, 12116 North Sycamore Street, Granville, Ohio. Just text yes or no to 554-343-1234 regarding your meeting availability. I will plan to meet you in the lobby at 11:50 a.m. and escort you to the office."

After Drew finishes reading the letter, he turns to Laura and lets her know that he plans to go with her. "There's no way I'm going to let you go to some stranger's office alone, especially with everything that's been happening to you lately."

At this point, it doesn't matter that the stranger had previously advised her not to tell anyone about their encounter. She is glad to have Drew accompany her.

So turning to him, she says, "You will get no argument out of me."

With her thoughts all over the place, Laura continues, "Honey, can this possibly be the same PI who is Officer Maloney's friend? Why does the name of the building where we are supposed to meet sound familiar? And the number one question that still haunts me is this—Is this stranger's news connected to everything that has been happening to me lately, including the planned car bomb?"

Still frazzled, Laura tries to clear her mind by fixing the full-course breakfast she had promised him. While beating the eggs, she recalls the memory that grabbed her attention earlier this morning and slowly turns to Drew, who is still sitting at the table.

"Honey, when I first saw this stranger, I knew there was something very familiar about him. He had an unusual limp that caused him to drag his left foot. Until this morning, I couldn't recall where I had previously seen him or at least someone with that type of limp. Now I remember.

"It was after my college graduation ceremony. I was walking out of the auditorium toward where Mama and other family members were proudly waiting. From out of the corner of my eye, I got a glimpse of a man who appeared to be limping toward me. As we briefly made eye contact, it looked like he was coming over to say something to me, but then one of my classmates came up to me and blocked our view. When I looked again, the man with the limp was nowhere to be seen. I'm not sure whether he changed his mind or if I was mistaken, but at the time, it sure looked like he was coming over to chat with me. Except for that unusual limp, I probably wouldn't have noticed him as we were all excited and ready to celebrate.

"Everyone was so proud of me as I was the first in my family to graduate from a four-year university, and that meant something special to the Parker family. You know, it's been twenty-five years since that graduation ceremony. I hadn't really thought too much about that man during all this time until the other week when I saw this stranger limping toward me. I know this may sound like a huge stretch of the imagination, but I have a weird feeling that it's the same man. Scary. Interesting."

Except for the clattering of dishes as Laura prepares to serve breakfast, everything is quiet. During breakfast time, they are absorbed in their private thoughts, trying to mask their feelings of uncertainty. Drew is thinking about everything she had just shared and wishing he could protect her from any unseen dangers. She is thinking about the father she never knew and how strange it is that everything seems to be converging at the same time. Then she thinks about the Father she does know and inwardly thanks Him for always being there for her. She can't help but smile. That smile reaches across the table to Drew, and although he doesn't understand why she's smiling, especially in spite of everything that's happening, he finds himself smiling too.

After giving her a hug, he tries to reassure her that it's going to be okay. Drew starts to clear the table while Laura uses his phone to text yes for the meeting scheduled for tomorrow. Not trusting their house phone, she calls Tina from Drew's phone, updating her on what they both had titled "the infamous stranger."

Before hanging up, Laura asks her for prayer.

"My friend, I'm already on it," she responds.

25

The hardest part about waiting for tomorrow is, well, just that, patiently waiting. Thinking back to when she was at the hotel and facing all sorts of craziness, she often still finds herself quoting, "Pray, renew your mind, pray. *Do not be anxious about anything, but in every situation, by prayer and petition, with thanksgiving, present your requests to God*" (Philippians 4:6 NIV). She does not fully understand why she gets such comfort from repeating this particular Scripture, but it continues to help her endure tough moments. She can hardly imagine what will happen when she learns to lean on so many more Scriptures.

Her mind goes back to Dr. Anderson's seminar and how she had spent a lot of time talking about the importance of renewing your mind. Laura has learned that the best way for her to renew her mind is to study the Bible. She remembers reading a Scripture that tells her *to cast down imagination and every high thing that exalts itself against the knowledge of God, and bringing into captivity any thought to the obedience of Christ* (2 Corinthians 10:5 KJV).

Basically, renewing my mind comes down to this—don't focus on anything negative. Instead, program my mind for positive thinking, Laura says to herself. Knowing this is more easily said than done, she picks up Dr. Anderson's book and turns to chapter 7 ("Why Own Your Worries?").

She reads, "It's so important not to dwell on the negative but to do as Jesus tells us—cast our cares on Him. He doesn't want us to worry about tomorrow for tomorrow will take care of itself. If you are fully persuaded of Who He is, you won't worry about tomorrow! If you are fully persuaded that your hope is in Jesus, you won't take ownership of your worries. If you are fully persuaded that He knows what He's doing, you won't go around with your head hanging down as one without hope! Simply put, if you are fully persuaded that He Who began a good work in you is well able to complete it, you will stop owning your worries. God will keep you in perfect peace if you keep your mind stayed on Him. Don't be in despair. Hide the Word of God in your heart so that you always have a reservoir that never runs dry.

"When trials, tribulations, and persecutions come, does your mind wander off into a place of disbelief, into a place of doubt, into a place of uncertainty? Or do you take comfort in the One Who is all of these things—the Mind Regulator, the Solid Rock, the Prince of Comfort, the Prince of Peace?"

Laura pauses for a moment and lets that information seep in. She admits to being a "work in progress." She knows she has a lot more to learn about renewing her mind. She knows that if she relies on her own abilities, which are very limited, she won't be able to do it. But she also knows that her struggles are not hers to bear, for God promises her that He will always be with her. So she's resolved to do whatever it takes to run this race one day at a time. Whatever happens tomorrow, there's one thing she can count on. God will still be in control.

Just as she's about to go downstairs to see what Drew is up to, the doorbell rings. She hears him as he greets the delivery person and is happy to hear that her new cell phone has arrived.

It's 5:00 a.m., and Laura is wide awake. Looking over at Drew, who is sleeping so peacefully beside her, she leans over and kisses him lightly on the forehead. Not trying to awake him, she quietly gets up out of bed without turning on the lamp. After picking up her Bible from the night-stand, she tiptoes into the guest room to spend some quiet time alone with God. With much apprehension regarding the upcoming meeting, she knows relying on strength and direction from God will be critical. So her devotion begins with a reading of the following Scriptures:

> *Trust in the Lord with all thine heart; and lean not unto thine own understanding. In all thy ways acknowledge Him, and He shall direct thy paths.* (Proverbs 3:5–6 KJV)

> *If any of you lack wisdom, let him ask of God, that giveth to all men liberally, and upbraideth not; and it shall be given him.* (James 1:5 KJV)

She sits there for a moment, just meditating on these Scriptures and allowing them to penetrate her mind. Then as she's about to pray, she recalls something that she had heard, either from Dr. Anderson or from Tina, "When you go to God in prayer, you don't need to use fancy words, no lengthy opening remarks or deep, thought-provoking closing arguments. Just a talk between your Father and you. As long as you are praying with a sincere heart, He hears it."

So she has a talk with her Heavenly Father, giving Him honor and praise for who He is. She thanks Him for His grace and His mercy. She thanks Him for her marriage and for bringing Drew safely home. She asks Him for wisdom and protection, not just for herself but for her family as well. She listens quietly for a moment, enjoying His presence. After a few more minutes, she ends her prayer by saying, "Not my will but Your will be done, in Jesus's name. Amen." She sits in silence for about ten more minutes. She enjoys being embraced by His presence.

Feeling strengthened by her talk with God, she returns to their bedroom and is surprised to see Drew awake, sitting up on the side of the bed and smiling to himself. Little does she know that while she was praying out loud, he had been standing outside in the hallway, listening to her every word.

Watching his facial expression, she gives him a puzzled look and says, "A penny for your thoughts." She anticipates he will mention something about the meeting, but instead, still smiling, he tells her that he too wants to strengthen his relationship with God. He tells her that he sees a change in her, and whatever it is that she has, he wants it too.

He gets up to hug her and continues, "I want us to walk this journey together with God at the front and center of our lives, for I know there's nothing we can't conquer together with God's help."

She is pleasantly surprised to hear him say these words; she can't resist the tears swelling up in her eyes. She gives a silent thanks to the Almighty God. Then with her arms still wrapped around Drew, she replies, "Me too, I want that more than anything!"

26

While they are eating breakfast around 8:30 a.m., their doorbell rings. It's the local police who are working alongside Officer Maloney on Laura's case. After the officer provides sufficient identification, she is invited inside, then begins to provide updates.

"As you know, due to the mitigating circumstances of your case, this investigation has been a joint effort between the police authorities and the Regal Bay Resort Hotel. Well, we are pleased to tell you that we have a breakthrough. Things have developed pretty quickly since you last heard from Officer Maloney. I believe he informed you yesterday that authorities were able to trace the bomb device to a shop in Texas. For quite some time, that shop had been under investigation for illegal sales, so it was already on our watch list.

"At any rate, the shop owner was able to provide camera footage. This footage included a photo of the customer who purchased the bomb device. Based on further investigation, we were able to link bomb device fingerprints to a suspect who has ties to that customer. I know this sounds farfetched. Our investigation uncovered that all of these individuals are paroled felons. They were hired to purchase and plant the bomb device.

"During separate interviews, we determined that their stories corroborated each other's. Our investigation uncovered that the bomb device purchased was not the type they were instructed to purchase. According to our sources, the suspects who placed the device underneath your car were hired by an unidentified person or persons. These person or persons never intended to have you murdered. Sources confirmed that the suspects were supposed to use a less powerful explosive device, only as a scare tactic.

"According to our sources, the hired suspects got greedy and attempted to get more money from whoever hired them. When their demands were not met, the suspects decided to rig the device to make it more powerful.

"I know this all may sound crazy, but if it's any consolation to you—and we know it probably isn't—based on information uncovered by our sources, it may not have been anyone's intent to have you murdered.

"We are expecting a breakthrough on whoever is behind this criminal plot at any minute now. Obviously, when it happens, we will get back with you immediately. In the meantime, until that happens, we believe it is necessary to maintain surveillance around your home. Accordingly, an officer will be in an unmarked vehicle close by for at least the next forty-eight hours."

Sure enough, when Drew peeps out through the window, there is an unmarked vehicle on the other side of their street. While this whole situation is scary and bizarre, they take some comfort in this precautionary measure and thank the officer. When the officer is preparing to leave, she gives them her card and asks that they contact her right away if anything comes up on their end.

Laura and Drew exchange glances, wondering silently whether to share anything about their pending meeting with the stranger. Seeing their facial expressions, the officer pauses and adds, "If there's any information you believe could possibly be critical to your case, now would be a good time to share it."

Laura isn't sure whether Officer Maloney has informed the authorities anything about her encounter with the stranger and, for a brief second, debates on whether they do so. However, since they aren't even sure if there is a connection, they don't want to complicate matters, especially since the stranger had asked her not to tell anyone about it. Looking at Drew, she shakes her head and, again, thanks the officer for the update.

After the officer leaves, they chat a little about whether or not they should have said anything about the stranger's meeting. Laura decides to call Officer Maloney for advice but gets his voice mail and leaves him a brief message.

Based on everything the officer just shared with them, Laura finds herself getting overly anxious. So since she still has a few minutes before she needs to get dressed, she goes upstairs and opens her Bible. She realizes that meditating on a couple of Scriptures will be medicine to her spirit. She loves reading passages where Jesus Himself is speaking, *These things I have spoken unto you, that in me ye might have peace. In the world ye shall have tribulation, but be of good cheer; I have overcome the world* (John 16:33 KJV). She turns to the Old Testament and recalls King David's words when he was feeling overwhelmed, *My flesh and my heart faileth, but God is the strength of my heart, and my portion for ever* (Psalm 73:26 KJV). Feeling somehow refreshed, she says a quick prayer of thanksgiving.

It's now 9:30 a.m. and time to get dressed for their pending meeting with the stranger.

The McIntire Building is only about forty minutes from their home, and since the meeting is scheduled for 11:50 a.m., they figure if they leave the house around 10:30 a.m., they should have ample time.

Just as they are about to pull out of their driveway, Laura gets a call from Officer Maloney. She turns on the speaker so Drew can listen.

"I'm returning your call but need to quickly ask you something. Does the name McIntire mean anything to you?" he asks.

Stunned, she tells him that they are on their way to the McIntire Building downtown, about forty minutes away from their home. She then tells him about the note that was left in their mailbox, and that they are scheduled to meet with the infamous stranger at 11:50 a.m.

"During our investigation, the name McIntire came up. At this time, we aren't sure what this means, if anything. I will tell you that things are moving rather quickly. It's amazing how much information suspects, especially paroled offenders, are willing to give up when they know they are facing more prison time!"

She then tells him that the police officer had dropped by earlier. They don't know if they should have mentioned anything about her encounter with the stranger. When she asks if he has said anything to them about it, he replies no, especially since he hasn't received her permission to do so. She tells him even though they want him to know about their pending meeting, they don't believe it is necessary to inform the police.

As an afterthought, Laura tells him that the note stated the stranger's name was PI Fletcher. She then asks him if his PI friend's name was Fletcher.

"No," he responds, "but I'll check with him to see if that name rings a bell."

They hang up after she promises to call him later.

They arrive at the McIntire Building around 11:25 a.m. As they are walking toward it from the parking lot, Laura can't help but notice the antique building's remarkable architectural design. The outside structure of the twenty-six-floor building is made up of elegant marble and stone with a gorgeous entryway of four tall white columns. There's a cascading water fountain that is surrounded by the most beautiful flower garden she has ever laid her eyes upon. There are stone benches on all sides of the fountain. The entire scene reminds her of an old historic Egyptian building. Elegant. Regal. Majestic. In her mind, it is the epitome of riches. Subconsciously, her focus on the building's design is an effort to keep her mind off the pending meeting.

Once inside the grand building, they are greeted by a concierge, who checks their identification, then escorts them to a lounge area. Drew squeezes her sweating hands and gives her a reassuring smile.

At exactly 11:50 a.m., the stranger approaches them. Nodding at them, he does not appear surprised at all to see Drew. He introduces himself as PI Fletcher and makes small chitchat. As they follow him to the elevator, seeing his limp takes her back in time to her graduation ceremony. While they are in the elevator, she cannot resist the urge to ask him whether he was, in fact, at her college graduation.

To which he pauses and looks clearly taken by surprise, he responds, "Let's talk about that in a few minutes."

The elevator stops on the nineteenth floor, and as they get off, the three of them are greeted by a mature-looking receptionist who escorts them into a conference room that has a large rich mahogany table with soft-leather matching chairs. In the far corner of the room, a refreshment buffet table is set up with an assortment of fruit, finger sandwiches, veggies, tea, and coffee. After the receptionist seats them, she leaves. A young waiter, probably in his late teens, is standing nearby the buffet. He offers them something to eat. Laura asks for tea, and Drew, coffee. Neither are hungry for food. They are both anxious for this meeting to start. Their thoughts are all over the place. Laura turns to the stranger to ask him another question, then seeing the set expression on his face, decides against it.

She's pretty confident that his reply will be the same as before. "Let's talk about that in a few minutes."

After what seems like forever, actually it's only been about ten minutes, the most distinguished-looking mature woman enters the room. She has an aging beauty, looks to be about sixty-four, and carries herself with such an air of authority that there's no doubt who is in charge whenever she is present. After taking a seat at the head of the table, with the stranger sitting to her right, she beckons for the waiter to bring her some tea and fruit. She asks if they are comfortable, thanks them for agreeing to the meeting, especially under the unusual circumstances. She then promises to answer any of their questions shortly. Finally, she introduces herself as Julia McIntire.

Laura can't help but steal a glance at Drew, who is holding her hand underneath the table. She is slowly making a connection that it's very likely this lady or at least someone in her family is extremely wealthy and possibly owns this building!

Acknowledging Drew's presence, Julia turns to Laura and says, "My dear, I am your father's youngest sister. Let me begin by stating that I knew nothing about your existence until a few months ago. And why I wouldn't blame you if you never believe me, according to your father, he did not know of your existence until that time either. I know…I know, but please hear me out before you pass judgment."

Laura is staring at the lady who just said, "I am your father's youngest sister." She's shaking her head, clearly confused by this statement.

How can this lady be my aunt? wonders a speechless Laura. She looks around the room, thinking maybe this is a game show, and cameras are rolling. Still shaking her head, she directs her attention back to this lady!

Frowning, Julia looks over at the stranger who calls himself PI Fletcher. Seeing that Laura seems to be confused and stunned, Julia continues, "I can imagine you have lots of questions. If I were in your shoes, my mind would also be brimming with all sorts of questions. May I assume you know very little about your father?"

To this, Laura simply nods.

"Well, you will be meeting him shortly. For now, he asked that I sort of set the stage for him. Basically, he's afraid you won't want to see him after all these many years. But I can assure you that's through no fault of his own." Again, she looks over disapprovingly at PI Fletcher.

Laura can't help but wonder about their seemingly weird relationship.

"Let me tell you what I know. In 1965, when you were born, your father was twenty-two years old and a rising part-time television personality. Our father, who closely scrutinized all of us, had also been in show business. Therefore, he felt it was only natural that his son, your father, followed in his footsteps. Our father was a very determined, stubborn businessman who did everything possible to help his son succeed in his own chosen profession.

"Well, your father started out in television commercials, then advanced to daytime soap operas. He met your mother, who was nineteen at the time. It wasn't until recent months after he learned of you that he informed me how the two of them met. He was on set at a production studio near your hometown in Tennessee. I'll let him fill in the blanks, but basically from what I gathered, he met your mother at a nearby restaurant where she was working as a waitress. Long story short, they dated for about six months and fell in love.

"Unfortunately, in the mid 1960s, society was not friendly toward an interracial couple. It didn't matter that your mother's complexion was light-skinned. It was still 1965, and they had to make every attempt to keep their relationship a secret. He knew our parents wouldn't approve of their relationship. Yet he loved her so much that he wanted to marry her regardless.

"The weekend after he last saw her, he had flown out to California to audition for this movie. Late one night, after a filming rehearsal, he was driving back to the hotel where the cast was staying. He was involved in a devastating head-on collision. That awful automobile accident landed him in a hospital in a coma for months. When he came out of the coma, he was paralyzed and suffering from severe memory loss. It was a while before the family even knew whether he would make it."

Julia looks at them and can easily tell that her story seems a bit overwhelming.

"Trust me, there is proof of everything I am telling you. Please let me continue... Now this is where it gets even more unbelievable. During the time that your father was lying in a hospital, your mother attempted to get a message to him regarding her pregnancy. When she couldn't reach him, she mailed a letter to the rehearsal studio where he was working. Unfortunately, your mother's letter, announcing her pregnancy, fell into the hands of my sister, Susan. She was ten years older than your father. She had always been very protective of him and, as I came to realize much later in life, not a very nice person. I am extremely ashamed to admit that she intentionally withheld your mother's letter. Why?

"Here's what I learned recently. Immediately after reading your mother's letter, Susan hired a private investigator. When she was informed about your mother's background, she became furious! She clearly disapproved of their interracial relationship. She believed their dating and especially the pregnancy would bring disgrace to the family's name. She also assumed it would damage his professional career as an actor. To make sure they didn't connect, Susan later sent a notice to your mother, claiming that your father had died. Ultimately, she became your mother's only contact for our family. She was in a position of influence and was able to somehow shield the truth from both of them. Now I simply can't tell you how she managed that, but I can tell you that she was always a very devious and resourceful person.

"Dear, please let me interject something that I believe is of extreme importance. I'm not naive enough to believe that racial prejudices don't exist today. Unfortunately, we still have a very long way to go. However, I sincerely want you to know that I don't share Susan's or our father's racial prejudices.

"After about one year, with the help of some incredibly well-paid doctors and physical therapists, your father recovered from the majority of his injuries.

"According to what he told me recently, when he got out of the hospital, he attempted several times to get in touch with your mother, still not knowing about her pregnancy. Susan, being extremely close to him, was handling his business and personal affairs. So she was always in a position to run interference.

"After a while, he assumed that your mother had moved on with her life. Eventually, he relocated overseas and had a successful career, starring in various movies. While there, he married and had two daughters.

"It was only until Susan became deathly ill a few months ago that she finally told your father what she had done. Needless to say, he was clearly upset with her and immediately asked for my help in arranging a meeting between the two of you."

27

Julia pauses, takes a sip of water, and glares a long time at PI Fletcher as if to intentionally make him uncomfortable. Then she gives him the signal to chime in.

"Laura, I am not really a private investigator, at least not in an official capacity. I am Paul Fletcher, your late Aunt Susan's husband. We got married before your father's accident. Regrettably, when Susan intercepted your mother's letter about her pregnancy, she confided in me and made me swear to keep it a secret. Later, when I told her that I felt guilty and wanted to tell your father, she became furious with me. She threatened that if I ever told anyone, she would divorce me and see to it that I never received any alimony. I married into the McIntire's wealth and had become accustomed to living large. So I am sorry to say that I allowed greed to rule against my better judgment. From the time Susan first told me about your mother's pregnancy until the time of her illness, our marriage had been one of greed, deceit, and lies. I know this is something that I'll have to live with for the rest of my life. I am so sorry. I realize I may never receive your forgiveness, but I want to make amends in any way possible. We have robbed you and your mother of so much, and that's inexcusable.

"When Susan became ill, she confessed all of this to your father and asked for his forgiveness. Around the same time, I finally got up enough nerve to tell Julia. I didn't want to delay any longer in letting her know.

"Also, if it is any consolation, Susan asked that I personally deliver a message to your mother and you. She knew that time was not on her side, and just in the unlikely event she wasn't able to handle this herself, she wanted me to do so. She was never a very religious person. But when she became extremely ill, she seized the opportunity to seek God's forgiveness and invited Him into her heart. Along with a priest, I was able to witness that moment. She so desperately wanted to make things right with you and your mother. She asked and received my forgiveness as well. Then she asked that I let you know how sorrowful she was for her actions. She hoped that you two would forgive her. She wanted to personally get a written letter to you before she died. But unfortunately, before she was able to write that letter, she slipped into a coma and died. Toward that end, I believed she truly regretted her actions. Hopefully, you will find it in your heart to forgive your aunt and to also pass this message on to your mother.

"Again, I'm so sorry for my part in all of this, but please believe this. From a distance, I always kept track of you. For example, it was me who sent you an anonymous monetary gift for your high school graduation. When you applied to Williams & McIntire University, without anyone's knowledge, I paid for your scholarship and asked that it remain anonymous. And yes, you've probably guessed it by now, Williams & McIntire University is an integral part of your family's heritage. It was later renamed after your great, great grandfather, Henry Scott McIntire, who, along with his friend, John Williams, had provided an enormous endowment to the school. Due to their generosity, the school was renamed in their honor.

"Yes, to answer your earlier question, you did see me at your college graduation. Against Susan's wishes and without anyone else's knowledge, I was determined to see you graduate, perhaps out of guilt or shame. Another example. Even though I didn't personally attend your wedding, I sent an anonymous monetary gift. By the way, I got an opportunity to see a copy of your beautiful wedding video. I never mentioned any of this to Susan or anyone else."

Suddenly, there is a flurry of activities all happening at the same time. Laura's cell phone rings, and the receptionist anxiously comes into the conference room with an urgent message for Julia. She rushes out, and Laura answers a call from Officer Maloney.

"Laura, we have two individuals in custody. They were attempting to flee the country when they were apprehended. Our sources reveal these two allegedly hired the suspects to bomb your vehicle. They also hired persons to perform other acts against you. These included spying on you, breaking into your room, and tapping into your phones. Other payments were for the interception of calls between your husband and you, posing as an imposter for the dean at your son's school and several other lesser offenses. Get this—these two suspects are sisters. Now would you like to take a guess at their last name?"

Before Laura gets a chance to respond, they are interrupted by Julia's abrupt and frantic return to the conference room. Rushing into the room, she looks toward Laura, and clearly bewildered, she exclaims, "Dear, I had no idea. I simply had no idea!"

Turning to Paul, who is now standing, she says, "You'd better tell me you had absolutely no warning about any of the awful attacks that have recently been carried out against Laura."

Puzzled and furiously shaking his head, he first looks at Laura and then Julia. "I have absolutely no idea what you are talking about. I can 100 percent promise you that I know nothing about any attacks carried out against her," he responds.

Just at that precise moment, an older, more distinguished, handsome man wearing glasses comes rushing into the conference room. He suddenly stops and stares at Laura. She doesn't seem to be able to take her eyes off him either. Seemingly, he's trying to decide whether to go directly to her or wait for an invitation. The man, after shaking his head, turns and glares at Paul Fletcher as if he will pounce on him at any moment.

While trying to absorb everything that is being said, a stunned Drew takes the phone from a trembling Laura. He hears Officer Maloney saying, "Laura, are you there? Did you hear anything I just said? Where are you? Are you okay?"

Drew responds and lets him know he has the phone on speaker now. Then he asks him to repeat what he just told

Laura as she is preoccupied with a lot of stuff going on in the conference room.

Total pandemonium in the room, Drew is trying to keep his eyes on Laura while listening to Officer Maloney. Julia is wobbly, looking like she's about to pass out, clearly upset about the news she just received. Paul is trying to get her to settle down while keeping one eye on the man who seems to want to do him bodily harm. That man is still staring at Laura. And the poor teen waiter, who has been nervously pacing back and forth near the buffet the entire time, watches the entire scene unfold as if in slow motion. He's trying to decide whether to stay for the final act or flee the scene entirely!

Drew turns up the volume on the speakerphone, which causes everyone to stop in their tracks.

Officer Maloney asks Laura, "Is it true that your father's name is Scott McIntire? If so, is it true that he has two other daughters? I ask you this because the suspects who were just apprehended at the airport are his daughters. If this is correct, I assume these are your sisters?"

Hearing all this and staring at the man who just entered behind Julia, Laura staggers to her feet, looks around at the others, starts to get dizzy, grabs at her temples as if to ward off a migraine headache, and grips the edge of the table to steady herself. She appears to be on the verge of another fainting spell. Drew catches her just in time and gently guides her to the nearest chair.

He looks in the direction where Laura is staring. Then he stares at the White man who is staring back at her. Wow! What a resemblance! Without a shadow of a doubt, Drew is confident that he's staring into the face of the man who is at the center of it all. He's staring at Scott McIntire, Laura's long-lost father! He's staring at one of the wealthiest men in the region.

Drew finally remembers that Officer Maloney is still on the phone. He thanks him for the update, lets him know that things are a little overwhelming for Laura at this time. He promises to call him back as soon as they leave the meeting.

Julia is accustomed to being in control. She doesn't like it when things become unrattled. So she finds herself in a very unusual position. Being so distraught, she turns to her brother Scott and asks if he wishes to continue the meeting. Even though he's filled with so many emotions, he also is a take charge person. So he tells Julia that he wants to spend some time alone with Laura and Drew. Taking that as a hint, Paul takes Julia by the elbow and escorts her out of the conference room. Scott also tells the waiter that he's free to leave as well.

Looking affectionately at Laura and Drew, he says, "Hello, guess you know by now that I'm Scott McIntire." To Laura, he adds, "My dear daughter, I cannot begin to tell you how elated it is to finally meet you. I am heartbroken for the awful set of circumstances that prevented us from meeting forty-seven years ago. I'm just as saddened and absolutely devastated to learn of the more recent events that are causing you pain and suffering. While I'm not fully aware of everything that's happened to you lately, I must admit that the limited amount of information I just received literally minutes before I walked through these doors leaves me shocked and ashamed.

While I was coming off the elevator and about to come into this room, I received a call from one of my daughters. She, along with her sister, are being held at the police headquarters near the Dallas / Fort Worth International Airport. I am almost at a loss for words!"

Apparently trying to pull himself together, he pauses, then says, "Is it okay if we leave this conference room for a less formal setting? My main home is in Texas, but because I come here quite often on business, I do have an apartment upstairs. It's quiet there, and we will have lots of privacy. Shall we leave?"

All Laura could do is look at Drew and nod her head. She's asking herself if this is a dream or reality.

Her father leads them out of the conference room toward the private elevator that takes them upstairs to his penthouse apartment. Once they are made comfortable, he offers the following information.

"Apparently, when my sister Susan informed me about the awful thing she had done, and that I had an older daughter, I was speechless. After getting over the initial shock and then the anger and bitterness, I thought it was only natural to share this news with my younger daughters. Never in a million years, did I imagine that they would plot to do whatever they could to harm you. Words can't express my feelings. I was clearly upset, horrified, and ashamed that my own daughters could be responsible for such inconceivable criminal acts against anyone!

"Now I realize what I'm about to share next won't lessen your pain or defend their actions. Perhaps one day, you will be able to find it in your heart to forgive them. I know that's asking a lot!

"You see, when they were preteens, their mother died of breast cancer. Because I traveled quite extensively, Susan volunteered to help rear them. Looking back, I realize leaving them in her care as often as I did was not in their best interest. Shamefully, due to her many racial biases, she helped to shape their prejudicial and discriminatory behaviors. How could I have been so blind? I ignored all the warning signs. Susan's racist attitude definitely had a negative impact on their lives. Additionally, I felt guilty for not giving them the amount of attention they so desperately needed. So I overly compensated by showering them with all sorts of materialistic things.

"Now because of my poor parenting decisions, I partially blame myself for the insidious acts of violence they perpetrated against you, their very own sister. Whether their actions were racially motivated or purely out of greed, I simply don't know. Does it matter? Probably not. I don't have the answers, but I gather they did not want to share their inheritance with you. Isn't that ironic. It's totally insane, and yet they were trying to make you out to be the one who was mentally unstable. As hard as I try, it's just too much to comprehend! Laura, I'm so sorry!"

28

Over the next few days, Laura and her father spend quite a bit of quality time together, catching up on life. They rotate visits between her home and his apartment. On occasion, Drew joins them, but he believes it's extremely important that the two of them have some alone time. So he encourages her to visit her father without him as often as she can. She and her father acknowledge this is just the beginning as they have forty-seven years of catching up to do.

In between visits with her father, Laura calls her mother, Becky, to see if this is a good week to visit her. Although they talk regularly on the phone, they haven't seen each other since the twins' college graduation last year. Becky seems eager for her to visit.

After Laura hangs up from speaking with Becky, she turns to Drew and says, "As shocking as this news is to me, I can't imagine what type of reaction she might have. So that's why I believe it's best to share it with her in person as soon as possible."

He agrees and asks if she wants him to accompany her on the flight to New York. She smiles adoringly at him and says yes.

As soon as Becky greets them at the airport, she senses Laura is hiding something. This raises suspicion, but she's thrilled to see them nonetheless.

Once they arrive at Becky's house, barely out of the car, Laura starts to share the news she has been most anxious to deliver. Without a doubt, Becky is stunned to learn that the first love of her life, Scott, is alive and well. Over the years, Laura had doubts whether Becky knew for certain if he was deceased. Now based on her reaction, Laura feels pretty confident she can put that doubt to rest.

She doesn't go into specifics because she believes it should be her father's place to provide more details about Susan's role in keeping them apart. However, she does mention that there were extenuating circumstances beyond her father's control. She adds that he wants to reach out to her but is concerned she may not believe his story. She asks her mother to trust her and to give him an opportunity to explain one of the most unbelievable stories that have ever been told.

After a few seconds of total silence, Becky starts to hyperventilate. Steadying herself, she gawks at Laura as if she has lost her mind. They make their way to the front door. Fumbling to unlock her door, Drew steps in, gently takes the keys from her, and unlocks it.

By this time, they have entered the house and are sitting in the living room. Drew goes to the kitchen and brings back a couple bottles of water.

Becky is shaking her head and mumbling, "Unbelievable, simply unbelievable." Then she asks Laura to repeat what she said earlier. Standing up and pacing around the room, she finally agrees that she will give him time to explain. She adds, "After all of these years, I'm doubtful that it will make a difference."

Then as if she just remembered something critical, turning to Laura with misty eyes, she says, "Now that you have met your father and his family, I assume you understand why I chose not to tell you anything about him when you were growing up. That was an extremely difficult time for me. I know what you must be thinking. Yes, once you became an adult, there were times when I wanted to respond to your many questions. But based on a lot of factors, I didn't think it mattered, especially since I thought your father was dead. I admit that was foolish and selfish of me. I truly hope one day, you will find it in your heart to forgive me."

Forgiveness. There's that word again. "Lord, help me," Laura mumbles underneath her breath. She is unsure how to respond to her mother's explanation for withholding such a critical piece of her heritage. At a loss for words, she looks at her and says, "Please let's talk more about this later. I still have lots of questions."

After lunch, as Drew catches up on business matters over the phone, the two of them talk some more. After dinner, there is more talking. They talk mostly through the night, barely getting any sleep.

Drew and Laura end up catching the red-eye return flight home, exhausted from their quick trip.

When they arrived home, Laura immediately calls her father and updates him on their visit with her mother. Scott doesn't waste any minute calling Becky. He knows time is no longer their friend.

When Laura contacts her father a few days afterward, he has this to share. "Yes, we talked over the phone, and while we both acknowledge it would be crazy to say we will pick up from where we left off, we can say with certainty that we have a much better appreciation of life. We still love each other and have agreed to take it one day at a time."

Laura smiles and says to herself, *That's all a daughter can ask.*

Three weeks later, Laura returns to her favorite riverbank escape spot. It's getting colder, and she has so much to do. This time, she doesn't plan to linger too long. Inhaling deeply, as she takes in the beautiful scenery, she can't help but thank God for all the many blessings in her life.

With her sisters' trial date pending, she tries to make sense of all the devious actions that were orchestrated by them. To think that they truly wanted to have her declared mentally unstable is something so mind-boggling that she decides not to dwell on it too much.

Yet in spite of all that has happened to her, she is most thankful for the protection of her Heavenly Father. She's thankful that He never, ever left her alone. He had given her the strength and faith to grow closer to Him. He had allowed her to come through it all unscathed and unharmed. Her marriage was strengthened, and she had finally met her long-lost dad after all these years.

Thinking of her dad, Laura is still having difficulties wrapping her mind around everything he shared with her during their first conversation after the conference room meeting. His words often replay in her mind. During that conversation, all Laura could do was stare at him and shake her head as she thought to herself, *Totally incomprehensible!*

Even now, she shivers when she thinks about her sisters and their actions. She's enjoying the scenic view and listening to the birds sing their songs. Yet in the midst of tranquility, her thoughts haven't strayed far from those two words *totally incomprehensible.*

Just before she turns to leave her favorite riverbank escape spot, she looks toward heaven and smiles, thinking about Mama. She knows Mama would have loved this tranquil, beautiful scenery. Just as quickly as this thought came to her mind, she smiles, looking upward again. For she knows that Mama's new eternal home is much more beautiful, peaceful, and indescribable than this place could ever become.

Back home, with the Thanksgiving holiday only one month away, Laura thinks this is a perfect time to extend a dinner invitation to her father and mother. Drew agrees. So she invites them and waits patiently for their response.

Laura had already told her sons about their grandfather and the reason why he hadn't been in her life. Initially, because the story seemed so unbelievable, they had reservations about meeting him. They still can't comprehend how their mother knew nothing about his background. How can she not know about such a critical piece of their family history?

However, after hearing how happy their mother is, regardless of the facts, they can't resist the temptation to learn more about him. And oh, by the way, who cares that their grandfather's last name just happens to be McIntire!

Laura also informs them how her stepsisters have attempted to drive her insane. She really doesn't want to tell them about the planned car bombing. However, Drew agrees that it is best if they hear it directly from them. They don't want them to hear it from the news media or other sources. Due to the McIntire family name, her bizarre story has made headlines, and reporters are all over the place, trying to get interviews with her.

Obviously, she has seen photos of her sisters in the newspapers, but she hasn't visited them in jail. Their bond has been denied due to possible flight risks. She has been doing a lot of praying lately, not just for herself but for their salvation as well.

She knows forgiving them for what they have done is key to her moving on.

"Lord, that's such a huge pill to swallow! I really need your strength to forgive them," prays Laura.

Then she hears a gentle sweet voice within her, *But if you do not **forgive** others their sins, your Father will not **forgive** your sins* (Matthew 6:15 NIV).

Wow! Then just as quickly, her mind goes back to something Dr. Anderson had said during the seminar, "Forgiving others might require an agonizing emotional struggle. It just might require fervent prayer on your part. But with the empowerment of the Holy Spirit, you can forgive."

As if to clear her head, she tries to reason with God, "Even this, Lord? Even this?"

Yes, she already knows God's answer. For she pictures the scene of Jesus kneeling in the garden of Gethsemane as He prays to the Father, "Not my will, but thy will be done." Then another scene flashes before her. Jesus painfully hanging on the cross and crying out, "Father, forgive them for they know not what they do."

Knowing what she must now do, she prays fervently for God's strength as she says, "Lord, not my will, but thine will be done in Jesus's name. Amen."

EPILOGUE

Five years later. Mostly during the autumn season, Laura, the girl from Chapel Hill, returns to her favorite escape place for a time of reflections. Laura stands still, admiring God's beautiful mountains and foliage. Much has happened during the five years since she rededicated her faith in her Heavenly Father, met her long-lost dad, and embraced her extended family.

Unlike five years earlier, when she came here with the stranger's news on the forefront of her mind, she now has a smile on her face and laughter in her heart. She stands tall with self-confidence and is fully persuaded of who she is. She embraces her God-given purpose in life. She does not take it lightly that God has given her a second chance to get it right. Laura's determination in saying, "Enough is enough," to being ruled by the battles within her is a daily process. She has gone from victim to victory, from trials to triumphs. She continues to lean on the God of yesterday, today, and tomorrow. She knows that He changes not but is more than able to change the hearts and minds of all who put their trust in Him.

Looking down at the tiny hands that are clinging tightly to hers, she smiles at her two-year-old granddaughter, Grace. When Marty and Danielle (his wife of three years) announced they were having a baby girl, Laura was thrilled to learn they had agreed to name her Grace after Mama. What a perfect name!

It is a couple of days before Thanksgiving, and the entire family has come home for the holidays. Everyone knows that little Grace, who is Laura's shadow, simply adores her grandmother. They all laugh when she follows her around the house while trying to say "Nana." As often as she can, Laura grabs the opportunity to spend time alone with her precious Grace. So here they are, just the two of them, hanging out at Nana's favorite riverbank spot and chatting as if they understand what the other is saying!

Whenever Laura sees Grace, she can't help but think about that other little girl, her own precious baby who is resting in the arms of Jesus. She is confident that she's in good hands, and that one day, the two of them will be reunited.

Laura does not take her blessings for granted. Her life is complete, and so she gives back by teaching others how to live a victorious life in Christ. Adoringly, Laura looks down at little Grace as she feels her tugging at her hands.

"I'll have to teach her the joy of patiently waiting," Laura says to herself. She looks forward to being able to teach Bible stories to her and other little children. She gets even more excited when she thinks about the possibility of more grandchildren coming her way. Matt and his fiancée are planning their wedding for next spring, and Laura's already talking about how she hopes they have twins and how much she looks forward to spoiling them all. She figures it will be a while before Mike settles down. He received his undergrad from Smithdeal-Madison University and is continuing his education at her alma mater, Williams & McIntire University.

Drew's new job doesn't require him to travel as much. So they enjoy spending more time together. They look forward to participating in weekly married couple's small group meetings at their church. Smiling, she thanks God for strengthening their marriage.

Looking back over her life, the victories and the disappointments, Laura can say with confidence that she is a better person today because of everything that happened to her. She's no longer teaching at Chestnut-Patterson University. Instead, she has finally embraced God's plan for her. She enjoys traveling to different places and conducting inspirational seminars mainly to an audience targeted toward college students. She finds herself eager to share her personal story, which she calls messages of triumph through faith, forgiveness, and freedom.

As often as opportunity allows, she shares her story with others who may need encouragement, urging them to pay it forward by sharing their own stories. She reminds them to embrace the measure of faith that God has freely given to each of them. She reminds them to readily forgive others, just as God has forgiven them. Finally, she encourages them to stand steadfast in their freedom and let no one persuade them otherwise.

Laura never forgets to pause and thank God for that week when her plans for a quick getaway of rest and relaxation at the Regal Bay Resort were "disrupted" by God's plans for her life. She is thinking as she often does about the many lessons learned from Dr. Anderson. She often thinks about how much those lessons lined up with the lessons she learned from Mama.

Laughing out loud, she kneels down and gently guides Grace's hands as she tries to throw small pebbles into the river. She smiles when thinking about how much Mama would have loved Grace, her namesake. She leans down and gathers Grace into her arms. Then the two of them exit her special riverbank place. In the car, Laura thinks about a song Mama used to often sing to her when she was a little girl. Trying to remember the words, she starts singing it to Grace who is buckled up in the backseat. "By grace, through faith, we are saved." Listening to Grace laugh out loud is priceless. Heading home, Laura's heart is filled with joy and gratitude.

The entire family is waiting. Life is waiting, and this girl from Chapel Hill wants to embrace every single moment of it.

A SPECIAL APPEAL FROM THE AUTHOR

Let me get right to the point because you've got things to do, places to go, and people to meet! So have you personally met Jesus yet? He has made such a major difference in my life, and He stands ready to do the same for you.

Do you know how much our Heavenly Father loves you? *For God so loved the world that he gave his one and only Son, that whoever believes in him shall not perish but have eternal life* (John 3:16 NIV). Yes, that's right! You are loved more than you can ever think or imagine!

I do not want to assume that you are confident where you will spend eternity. At the end of the day, when you've breathed your last breath or when Jesus returns, what will be your final destination? If you haven't accepted Him as your Savior, it is not too late. If you are not 100 percent sure you will spend eternity in heaven, this appeal is for you. Right now, wherever you are, Jesus stands ready with open arms to welcome you home.

There is only one way to God, and that's through His Son, Jesus Christ.

Jesus saith unto him, I am the way, the truth, and the life: no man cometh unto the Father, but by me. (John 14:6 KJV)

Neither is there salvation in any other: for there is none other name under heaven given among men, whereby we must be saved. (Acts 4:12 KJV)

Have you made the confession that Jesus Christ is Lord?

That if thou shalt confess with thy mouth the Lord Jesus, and shalt believe in thine heart that God hath raised him from the dead, thou shalt be saved. (Romans 10:9 KJV)

1. Admit that you are a sinner.

    As it is written, there is none righteous, no, not one. (Romans 3:10 KJV)

2. Be willing to turn from sin (repent).
3. Believe that Jesus Christ died for you, was buried and rose from the dead.

    For with the heart man believeth unto righteousness; and with the mouth confession is made unto salvation. (Romans 10:10 KJV)

4. Through prayer, invite Jesus into your life to become your personal Savior.

For whosoever shall call upon the name of the Lord shall be saved. (Romans 10:13 KJV)

If you haven't done so, now is the perfect time to accept Jesus as your personal Savior. A wonderful new life awaits you. So please stop what you are doing and repeat the following prayer.

A SIMPLE PRAYER
OF SALVATION

Dear God, I am a sinner and need forgiveness. I believe that You sent Your Son Jesus Christ to shed His precious blood on the cross. I am willing to turn from sin. I ask for Your forgiveness. I thank You for forgiving me of all my sins. I confess with my mouth the Lord Jesus. I believe in my heart that You raised Him from the dead. So now, God, I invite Jesus Christ to come into my heart as my personal Savior. Amen.

As a monumental keepsake of your decision, feel free to sign your name on the space provided below. Most importantly, your name is written in the Lamb's book of Life (Revelation 13:8).

_____   _____
            Date   Signature

The End

ABOUT THE AUTHOR

Vanester M. Williams has been a minister of the Gospel of Jesus Christ for over twenty years. She is a host/ speaker on a weekly broadcast called *His Abounding Grace*, a program under the ministry of *When Christians Speak Talk Radio*. She has served as a Sunday school teacher, pulpit and conference speaker, and administrator. She is passionate about encouraging others and teaching them how to strengthen their Christian journey. She is a retiree of the US Federal Government and holds a degree in biblical studies and a certificate in biblical counseling principles. She is a member of Lifepoint Church, Fredericksburg, Virginia, where she serves as a group leader. She enjoys reading, writing, and family gatherings. She and her husband, Rick, have been married for over forty-five years. They are the proud parents of two grown children, two grandchildren, and several godchildren. They enjoy each other's company and happily reside in Fredericksburg, Virginia.